# Connecticut
## State Facts

| | |
|---|---|
| **Nicknames:** | Constitution State, Nutmeg State, Provision State |
| **Date Entered Union:** | January 9, 1788 (the 5th state) |
| **Motto:** | *Qui transtulit sustinet* (He who transplanted still sustains) |
| **Connecticut Men:** | P. T. Barnum, *showman* Charles Goodyear, *inventor* Noah Webster, *lexicographer* Samuel Colt, *inventor* |
| **Flower:** | Mountain laurel |
| **Tree:** | White oak |
| **Bird:** | American robin |
| **Song:** | "Yankee Doodle" |
| **State Name's Origin:** | Based on Mohican and Algonquin Indian words for a "place beside a long river." |
| **Fun Fact:** | In Hartford you may not, under any circumstances, cross the street walking on your hands! |

### "This isn't finished, Hayley. Not by a long shot."

Hayley tried not to think how right Dillon's lips felt on hers. "I'm not sure I'll ever be ready for a love affair with you, Dillon."

"Then I'll be disappointed." He kissed her brow lightly and hugged her close. "We've got incredible chemistry, Hayley. It'd be a crime to waste it."

"It'd be more of a crime to begin something wildly satisfying that we know is only going to end," she replied.

"No, Hayley," Dillon said, cupping her chin and bringing her mouth to his. "It's more of a crime not to experience it at all."

# American
# HEROES
## AGAINST ALL ODDS

## CATHY GILLEN
# THACKER
## Honeymoon for Hire

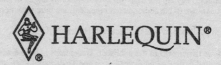

# HARLEQUIN®

TORONTO • NEW YORK • LONDON
AMSTERDAM • PARIS • SYDNEY • HAMBURG
STOCKHOLM • ATHENS • TOKYO • MILAN • MADRID
PRAGUE • WARSAW • BUDAPEST • AUCKLAND

**HARLEQUIN BOOKS**
225 Duncan Mill Road, Don Mills,
Ontario, Canada M3B 3K9

ISBN 0-373-82205-7

HONEYMOON FOR HIRE

# About the Author

**Cathy Gillen Thacker** is a full-time wife/mother/author who began typing stories for her own amusement during "nap time" when her children were toddlers. Over twenty years and more than fifty published novels later, Cathy is almost as well-known for her witty romantic comedies and warm, family stories as she is for her ability to get grass stains and red clay out of almost anything, her triple-layer brownies, and her knack for knowing what her three grown and nearly grown children are up to almost before they do! Her books have made numerous appearances on bestseller lists and are now published in seventeen languages and thirty-five countries around the world.

**Books by Cathy Gillen Thacker**

Harlequin American Romance

Dear Reader,

My husband and I have lived in eight different places in the course of our marriage. It didn't really matter where we lived, or how big or small the home was, as long as we were together.

Yet I must confess that when the children came along, we began to yearn for a house with a yard and a swing set for the children to play on. A place where we could have a dog, and the kids could ride their bikes.

So when New York City heroine Hayley Alexander began to want the same thing for her baby in *Honeymoon for Hire*, I knew she would want to live in nearby Connecticut. In a pretty neighborhood filled with big Colonial homes, and beautiful green lawns, and lots of other families and kids.

The only problem is, Hayley—a young widow—can't afford to buy a house like that on her own. So she does the next best thing. She takes a job as a live-in housekeeper for sexy newsman, Dillon Gallagher.

Naturally, nothing is ever as simple as it seems...and before Hayley knows it, she and Dillon are entering into an equally convenient "marriage," with none of the usual benefits.

I hope you enjoy reading this as much as I enjoyed writing it.

Best wishes,

*Cathy Gillen Thacker*

Please address questions and book requests to:
Harlequin Reader Service
U.S.: 3010 Walden Ave., P.O. Box 1325, Buffalo, NY 14269
Canadian: P.O. Box 609, Fort Erie, Ont. L2A 5X3

# Chapter One

Hayley Alexander sized Dillon up with street smart expertise, ran a hand through the thick waves of her honey blond hair and let out a short exasperated sigh. "Look, Mr. Gallagher, I appreciate your dropping by, but if you've come to do the 'merry widow' routine on me, you can forget it. I'm much too busy subletting my apartment, looking for a job, and finding a new place to live to mess with the likes of you. So let's do both ourselves a favor and make it short."

"Like I could get a word in edgewise," Dillon drawled.

"You're sorry. I'm sorry. Thank you. And goodbye." She punctuated each short sentence with a decisive wave of her hands, then started to palm the door shut on him.

Dillon caught the edge of the door to her pricey New York City apartment and held firm' easily preventing her from shutting it. "Whoa, babe."

"And don't call me babe," she snapped archly.

He'd had a feeling she wouldn't like that, no more than he liked taking the blame for something he hadn't been about to do. "I don't know what this merry widow routine is—"

"You don't?" Her jade green eyes widened in cool disbelief.

"No, sweetheart, I don't," he replied.

Dark green eyes flashing, she took a deep breath to bolster her determination. "Then let me spell it out for you," she said.

Dillon let go of the door and propped his spine against the jamb. Slouching slightly to better align his six-foot-three frame with her five-foot-eight height, he crossed his arms against his chest. "Considering how riled up it gets you, I can't wait to hear."

She pursed her incredibly soft-looking lips together and shot him a drop-dead look that in no way detracted from her femininity. "Are you going to take me seriously, Mr. Gallagher?"

That was a hard one to answer, considering she was mad at him for no reason at all.

"'Cause if you're not—" she warned.

"Then what?" It had been a long time since he'd seen a woman with such spunk and vitality. Too long, he decided.

She sighed and rolled her eyes. "You NCN News guys are all alike."

"Tell me about it," he urged with an insolent grin.

"I'm a lady. I don't use obscene language."

He laughed. "I take it I'm not your first visitor?" he teased.

"Since the Gulf War ended, there've been twenty-two of you. You, Mr. Gallagher, make it twenty-three."

That revealed, she turned her back on him and marched toward the kitchenette at the other end of the cluttered, overcrowded living room. Dillon followed, striding past a nubby oatmeal sofa, an easel, two eye-catching paintings of bunny rabbits and teddy bears, and a baby carriage heaped with clean laundry. "Let's get back to the merry widow routine. What exactly is that?"

She picked up a wrench and restlessly cupped it in both slender hands. "Oh, you know, it's where you come in and tell me how sorry you are Hank died last year—"

Sounded reasonable, Dillon thought. That *was* why he was here.

"And now that you're back in the States, you just want me to know you're here for me. I'm not sure," she intoned dryly, "but I *think* that's the part where I'm supposed to wail and act helpless. But I gotta tell you, Dillon," she said, "I usually don't. Then you take me in your arms and make a pass."

Hayley began disassembling the faucet. "I don't know what it is about widows, but damned if everyone doesn't think we're a sex-starved lot."

Dillon couldn't help it. He laughed. Bracing his hips against the other end of her kitchen counter, he said, "I assure you, Mrs. Alexander, I am not here to make a pass." Although he'd damn sure like to be, he thought. Hayley Alexander was one sexy woman.

"So why *are* you here?"

Dillon edged closer, wishing he knew enough about plumbing to offer to lend her a hand. "I thought I'd stop by and see if there's anything I could do for you, because I cared about Hank." He paused, thinking briefly about the loss they'd both suffered. "I would've come sooner, but as you've already figured out, I just got back in the States myself."

Hayley stood on tiptoe and put her weight behind the wrench to turn it.

"You don't believe that's all there is to it, do you?" Dillon asked when she continued to concentrate on her task. He wasn't used to being ignored by women, period, and especially not pretty young ones.

She sighed. "The words are nice. My past experiences with NCN News guys says otherwise."

"They all made passes at you?"

"Twenty-one of them," she said flatly.

"Which is reason enough to be wary," Dillon added pragmatically. "But it doesn't surprise me that a lot of your husband's colleagues would want to make a condolence call. Hank was respected. As for the passes—" Dillon sighed ruefully "—what can I say? I'm sorry anyone made you uncomfortable. On the other hand, let's face it. You are a very beautiful woman and—"

"And what?" she interrupted. She faced him, hands on her slender hips. "Because I have looks, men aren't responsible for keeping their hands to themselves?"

"Not at all," Dillon said, trying hard not to notice how the preemptive action had drawn her blouse against her breasts.

Waving her wrench around dangerously to emphasize her point, she advanced on him. "I am not lonely, Dillon Gallagher. Contrary to popular opinion, I am *not* hot to trot! So try spreading *that* around NCN, would you please?"

Dillon chuckled and capturing the wrench from her hand, lowered it to waist level before she did any damage with it, and held it between them. "Watch where you're swinging that thing, would you?" Dillon asked, tightening his grip on her hand.

If she weren't careful, she'd be swinging it below his belt. He didn't need any more pain in that area; the ache he had from just looking at her was torment enough.

"Sorry." Hayley had the grace to look embarrassed for her outburst. "I've just had enough tea and sympathy to last me a lifetime, you know?"

"I know."

"I want to get on with my life."

"You should."

"Out of Manhattan. Somewhere safer, where Christine can have plenty of fresh air and sunshine, and a backyard to play in and plenty of friends her own age."

"Sounds like a reasonable goal." Even if that kind of life wasn't for him, he thought. "As long as I'm here, is there anything I can do to help you?"

"Thanks for the offer," Hayley said. She turned and went back to her faucet. "But as you can see, I'm getting along fine."

*More than fine,* Dillon thought, as he watched her replace the washers.

He knew she'd just given him his cue to leave, but oddly enough, he wasn't ready. And his wanting to stay had nothing to do with the way she looked in those close-fitting ivory leggings and that stylish thigh-skimming tangerine top. He just wanted to see she was all right. "Where are you moving to?"

Hayley frowned as she began to put the faucet back together again. "I don't know yet. It will depend on where I get a job."

"You're a financial analyst, aren't you?" The last he had heard, she'd worked for a high-profile Wall Street firm.

"Yes," Hayley admitted, "but I'm not going back to it."

"Why not?"

"Christine. I don't want to leave her with a sitter all day." Hayley knelt down to turn the incoming water back on. Straightening, she turned the tap on. Water came out in a steady stream.

"You could free-lance and work out of your home."

"I know—"

"But?"

"I just went into the field because it would allow me to make a good living, but I hated the work."

"So, what do you want to do?"

"Illustrate children's books."

That explained the paintings of teddy bears and bunnies he'd seen.

"Unfortunately I haven't got the writing talent to go with it. So I'll either have to find a partner who can write but not draw, or get hired as a free-lance illustrator by a publisher here in the city."

"I've got a few friends in the business," Dillon offered, finally seeing a way he could ease his guilt about what had happened to Hank. Though everyone had told him, from the lowliest camera grip to the chief of the network, that Hank's death wasn't Dillon's fault. "Maybe I could help—"

"No." She cut him off, her voice unexpectedly sharp. "Thanks." Taking a deep breath, she softened her voice with obvious effort, "I do it on my own or I don't do it."

"All right." He watched her replace her tools in the metal box on the counter. "Don't you have a super who takes care of things like that for you?"

"I can take care of myself."

"So I've noticed," Dillon drawled.

In the distance there was some shuffling and then a thud, followed by the sound of a baby's happy gurgling. Hayley's face lit up. "That's Christine." Her infectious smile widened. "Would you like to see her before you leave?"

Dillon hesitated. He didn't know anything about babies, but not wanting to insult her, he nodded. "Sure."

He waited in the hall. Hayley returned a moment later, balancing the baby on her hip. "This is Christine."

Dillon stared at Hayley's daughter, searching for something to say. "She's beautiful," he said finally, because it was true. Christine had Hayley's same naturally curly, honey blond hair, heart-shaped face and dark green eyes with long gold-tipped lashes.

"I think so, too," Hayley admitted, casting an adoring look at her baby daughter.

Dillon glanced at his watch. "Well, I'd better get going. I've got to interview some housekeeper over in Bridgeport." Not that he actually intended to hire the old battle-ax, he thought. He was just going through the motions to humor his sister, Marge.

"For your family?" Hayley asked.

"For me," Dillon specified, wanting her clear on that much. "I'm single. And the next few months are probably going to be sheer hell, as I try to get settled. I'm moving back to the States, after twenty years of living abroad."

"You don't sound happy about it."

Dillon shrugged. "I don't really want to work in New York again."

"Too much crime?"

"Too dull. But the job was a step up, USA Bureau chief for NCN, Northeastern Cable News. So I told 'em I'd give it a try for one year."

"And then?"

Dillon shrugged, knowing the management experience there was going to be worth its weight in gold to him later. "If I don't like it, I'll head back to the Middle East."

"You sound like you think you won't like it," Hayley said, her brow arching in disapproval.

Dillon wasn't about to apologize for his lack of domesticity or his love of adventure. "I'm going to give it my best shot." He frowned. "It's the house that I let my sister talk me into buying that I'm really uneasy about. It needs a hell of a lot of work to make it habitable, or so I've been told. I haven't actually seen anything but pictures to date.''

Jade eyes sparkling, Hayley grinned and shook her head in silent bemusement. ''Sight unseen, hmm?''

''Yep.''

''So why'd you buy it?''

''The investment, of course.''

''Of course,'' Hayley said dryly.

''I'm planning to resell it at the end of a year's time, when my assignment is up, and make a killing.''

''So where is this house?'' she asked.

''Connecticut.''

''Connecticut,'' she murmured wistfully. ''I've always wanted to live there.''

Something about her expression, kind of like a kid with no money looking hungrily through the glass at the candy counter, got to him. It made him—he told himself firmly it was for Hank's sake only he was feeling this way— want to make it possible for her to get exactly what she wanted. ''Say,'' Dillon said casually. ''You wouldn't be interested in the job as my housekeeper, would you?''

She merely rolled her eyes at the suggestion. ''Thanks, but there's no way I could commute back and forth from the city every day.''

Dillon shrugged, not so willing to be dismissed, even if his idea was a little crazy. ''So you and the baby could live in,'' he persisted. ''Think about it. You'd have another entire *year* to get your future sorted out.''

She laughed, a rich melodious sound. ''You're kidding. Right?''

''No,'' Dillon said. ''You need a job, preferably one that will allow you a lot of time to spend with your baby, which mine will, and a nice safe place to live. You're handy with a wrench. You seem to have a fair amount of decorating skill. At least I like what you've done with this place, sans moving boxes, anyway. You're just what I need to make my house habitable. And my house is just the kind of place you need to raise your baby in and regroup.''

''Thanks, but I'm not interested in being anyone's maid. I have enough trouble just cleaning up my own messes.''

''Hey, I'm not that messy,'' Dillon protested automatically. Her delicate brow arched. He continued, ''Besides, you'd be a lot more. You'd be decorating, organizing all my stuff, creating order out of chaos, making a home for me.'' He grinned mischievously. ''Or at least enough of one to get my sister off my back.''

''Your sister?'' Hayley blinked.

''Marge.'' Dillon's mouth curved fondly at the thought of the sister he loved. ''She thinks I've ruined my life, and she wants me to settle down for at least a year and try to have a real life, one that includes more than just my work.''

Hayley wrinkled her nose. ''It sounds like what she really thinks you need is a wife.''

''Yeah,'' he agreed. ''Only thing is I'm not interested in getting married.''

''Well,'' Hayley said pragmatically with a sigh, ''that makes two of us.''

''So how about the job?'' Dillon tried to imagine what it would be like to have a woman as beautiful as Hayley working as his housekeeper. Bringing him his paper in the morning, making him breakfast... Maybe he'd even get a glimpse of her in some sort of negligee and robe, if they were under the same roof.

"Think about the time it would give you with Christine," he said persuasively. He figured he could handle a good-looking woman with a baby under his roof a lot better than he could handle the mustached, overweight, drill sergeant of a housekeeper his sister was pushing him to hire. Employing Hayley would ease his own guilt over Hank considerably. Even if he found her incredibly desirable, he wouldn't act on that desire because of his past friendship with Hank.

"Dillon, listen to me," she said with weary tolerance. "I know you think you're trying to help, but my schedule is erratic at best these days. I sleep when the baby sleeps. I'm awake when she's awake, even if that's from three in the morning until dawn. I don't know if I could have dinner on the table precisely at eight every night. Or even be awake enough to cook for you if you decided to have a dinner party."

"I never give dinner parties," he said flatly. "I only go to them. And as for schedules, my hours are erratic at best, too. Some nights I probably won't show up for dinner at all."

"Well, then I would be ticked off. If I went to all the trouble to cook the damned meal, I'd expect you to eat it."

He grinned at her feisty tone, liking the warm flush of color that had come into her cheeks. "I knew there was something I liked about you," he drawled.

They stared at each other in contemplative silence.

"What about salary?"

"What's fair?" Dillon volleyed back, mirroring her own pragmatic, let's-get-down-to-brass-tacks tone. "Room, board and say…ten percent of the profit I make when I sell the house at the end of a year? It's not as if you don't know me," he continued when she hesitated.

"True. Hank spoke of you often. He said you were a well-loved boss, respected by all who worked for you."

Which made his own betrayal of Hank all the harder to bear, Dillon thought. He should've known better than to have sent Hank into the fray. But how could he have known the barracks would be hit by shrapnel from an exploding missile? Dillon sighed.

Hayley was silent. Whether she was blaming him or not, Dillon couldn't tell. Finally she smiled. "I guess I can trust you."

Dillon grinned back. "Now you're talking."

"Add a monthly stipend of four hundred dollars for my personal expenses and you've got yourself a deal."

"Four hundred!" he echoed, stunned.

"Do we have a deal or don't we?"

*Damn but she was impulsive,* he thought. Almost as impulsive as he was. And she drove a hard bargain. But what did it matter whether they thought about this for ten minutes or ten days, as long as it solved all their mutual problems, which it did. Dillon studied her with satisfaction, realizing it had been easier for him to take care of both his own guilt and Hank's widow than he'd ever imagined it could be. "Okay, you're hired."

# Chapter Two

"You forgot one thing, Dillon," Hayley said, looking into his dark blue eyes and ruggedly handsome face with all the directness she could muster.

"Oh, yeah, what's that?"

"You didn't tell me I'd be moving into an absolute disaster," Hayley said, early the following morning.

Dillon frowned at the red walls and red velvet furniture in the formal living room. "I didn't know it was this bad," he said grimly, looking no more pleased than she felt.

Hayley sent him a skeptical glance as they trudged through the adjacent kitchen, which was decorated in shades of avocado and lemon yellow. "How is that possible?" she asked disbelievingly. "After all, you bought this house."

"No," he said with a flash of white teeth, "my sister did."

Hayley stopped him before he could head up the stairs to the second floor of the sprawling, white brick Colonial. *"You bought this house without at least seeing a detailed report of everything it would need to make it livable?"* she asked, incredulous.

"Right." Dillon glanced thoughtfully up at the chandelier overhead, which was coated with several years' worth of dust and spider webs.

Hayley kept her eyes trained on his face. He didn't look like an idiot. He looked smart, strong and sexy. *Too sexy,* she thought, her eyes roving over his tall, solidly built frame and broad, powerful shoulders. She hadn't been attracted to a man since Hank's death, but she was attracted to Dillon. And she felt that sizzle of attraction with heart-stopping awareness every time she looked into his mesmerizing dark blue eyes. "Why?"

"Why not?" Dillon shrugged. He tested the wooden banister and found it as wobbly as it looked. His glance met hers again. "I had no interest in trotting through home after home. One place is as good as the next as far as I'm concerned, so I decided to let my sister, Marge, handle the actual selection. That way, I already had a place when I got back to the States. All I had to do was wait for my stuff to arrive, find someone to unpack it and move in. Then she found this place, said it needed redecorating. A hell of a lot of redecorating. But it was a great bargain. So, shrewd investor that I am, I figured I'd capitalize on the financial opportunity."

"She didn't tell you it looked like a highly disorganized white elephant sale inside?"

"No. She said nothing about it being furnished like a clearance sale at an outdoor flea market." Dillon shoved a hand through the tousled, two-inch-long layers of his dark brown hair and shook his head. "In terms of redecorating, I figured I'd have to pick out new paint, wallpaper and carpet. Worst case, maybe even fix some of the plumbing. Which, of course, is why I hired you."

"Because you didn't want to mess with it," Hayley assumed.

"Not in this lifetime." Dillon affirmed her guess with a tantalizing grin.

So he hated decorating, Hayley thought. Most men did. He did pick out his clothes well. The brown Harris tweed jacket and dark brown trousers not only fit his muscular body well, they complemented his dark brown hair and suntan.

"But I have to admit, Hayley, this—" Dillon took a deep, bracing breath as he looked around him "—is just ridiculous, even for someone like me who really doesn't care where they live. If you want to back out—"

Hayley wasn't going to let him discourage her. It didn't matter to her the house was wrecked or that he was close enough to her in age and ruggedly good-looking enough to give her pause. All that mattered to her was the eventual cut of the profits it would bring. With that, she could make herself and Christine a real home. "Dillon, we'll fix it up."

"I'm not sure that's possible."

Hayley laughed softly. "Sure it is," she persisted, her artist's eye already seeing the potential beneath the disastrously decorated interior, even if he couldn't begin to. Whether Dillon could see it or not, this was the kind of house in just the kind of place that Hayley had always dreamed of living in. If only this were hers, she would've really arrived. It irked her that Dillon took for granted what she wanted most. And it baffled her that he was so disinterested in this kind of life that he hadn't even bothered to see the house he was buying.

She knew if she'd seen the pictures of the exterior of the majestic two-story Colonial on the serene, tree-lined drive she would've broken land speed records getting here! And to know it was hers...all hers. That would be heaven.

Well, Dillon might not care much for this kind of well-to-do suburban life-style, but she did. And she was going to enjoy every second she was here. Just as she would use the profits they made on the sale of the house for the down payment on a home for herself and Christine.

It wouldn't be nearly as grand as Dillon's home, of course. But it would be *theirs*. And it would be loved and cared for, by both herself and Christine.

"You'll feel differently about this house once it's cleaned up and redecorated," Hayley promised as Dillon continued to scowl at their surroundings. She could envision it now—with plush carpeting and freshly painted walls, plenty of sunlight pouring in...

"Don't try and humor me, Hayley," Dillon retorted, unappeased. "This place ranks with some of the tackiest places in the eastern hemisphere. And I oughta know— for the last twenty years I lived in them."

"Hello!" a chirpy voice called. A tall slim woman with cropped dark brown hair stepped through the door.

"Hayley, meet my sister, Marge. The *genius* who selected this place."

Marge strode forward to give him a quick hug. "I knew you'd be overwhelmed," she said, smoothing down the fabric of her green plaid skirt and coordinating turtleneck sweater. "Which is precisely why I didn't send you any pictures except of the outside."

Which Hayley admitted to herself didn't look too bad. The exterior had already been painted a gleaming white, with dark pine green shutters and a glossy black front door.

"What in blazes happened here?" Dillon demanded.

"Look, Dillon, this place does have its advantages," Hayley interjected.

"Such as?"

"An excellent floor plan, spacious rooms, a large yard with plenty of trees and beds for flowers in a wonderful neighborhood." It was a great place to raise Christine.

Marge smiled at Hayley, pleased someone had seen what she had in the place. "Hey, thanks." She paused as the sound of a baby's soft nonsensical chatter echoed through the first floor.

"Oh, that's my baby, Christine. She's in the stroller in the next room. She fell asleep while Dillon was showing me around, and we left her in there so as not to disturb her with our chatter.

Marge smiled. "How old is she?"

"Eleven months, last week."

"Would you mind if I went in to see her?"

"Actually, you could do me a favor and wheel her in here."

Dillon and Hayley picked up where they left off. "If the mess bothers you, why didn't you demand they at least clean it up first?" Hayley asked Dillon.

"Marge said I should take it as is and get another five percent off the already low purchase price, rather than pay the bank to oversee the cleaning of it. At the time the decision made sense." Dillon grimaced. "Now I don't know."

"Marge was right," Hayley agreed. She looked at the sofa and saw how sturdily it was built. The crushed red velvet could be removed. So could the black tassel fringe. "This way you can sort through everything yourself, figure out what's usable."

"For what? Starting a bonfire?"

Hayley grinned. "You'd be surprised what recovering a sofa can do. Besides, you're going to need plenty of furniture. This place is huge."

"Forty-five hundred square feet," Dillon remarked proudly.

"And don't worry about the decor," she assured him as they continued to walk around shoulder-to-shoulder. "That too, can be fixed." Hayley stopped and turned to face him. She had to tilt her head back to see his face. Both his height and their closeness were disconcerting to her. As was her potent reaction to his attractiveness. Every time she was near him, her heart beat a little faster, her senses got a little sharper, the loneliness she'd felt since Hank's death became more acute. "Not much of a visionary, are you?" she teased, wishing all the while he weren't quite so handsome and intelligent and kind.

"Not when it comes to domestic stuff," Dillon admitted.

Deciding she'd looked into his dark blue eyes quite long enough, Hayley turned away from Dillon once again. "Well, at least it's got the most important feature built-in," she remarked as she checked out the heavy, moth-eaten drapes.

"Indoor heating?" Dillon hazarded a droll guess.

"Two master bedroom suites with their own bathrooms. That'll give us both maximum privacy. We won't have to see each other running around in our pajamas."

Briefly Dillon felt disappointed. "Well, as long as you're sure I haven't made the biggest mistake of my life investing my life savings in this dump," he said dryly, "I guess all's well."

"It's not as bad as you think it is," Hayley said.

"Come on, Hayley, don't patronize me." Dillon stopped in front of the fieldstone hearth in the living room. "Even I know a little paint and elbow grease can't fix this place."

Hayley grinned, not disagreeing. "So we'll start from scratch."

"No, you'll start from scratch," Dillon reminded. "I want nothing to do with it. I don't so much as want to be shown a paint chip. 'Course, I'm handy at some things around the house." Dillon leered at her comically, leaving no doubt in her mind as to which room his thoughts were in.

"Save the bedroom antics," Hayley advised, her voice a little sharper than she intended. "I'm immune."

Dillon snapped his fingers and humorously feigned distress. "Darn." His eyes met hers, held. "No fringe benefits, hmm?"

"Not a one," Hayley said, spelling out the rules bluntly. She might be attracted to him, but she wasn't a fool. It would be hard enough living here with him in such a wonderful place, knowing it would never really be hers, without starting a love affair.

Footsteps sounded in the hall. Marge came in, carrying Christine in one arm, pushing the stroller with the other. Marge looked as smitten as her daughter. "I guess we don't have to ask if the two of you got on all right," Hayley said.

Marge smiled warmly at Hayley before turning once more to her brother. "You could still introduce me more properly to our friends, Dillon."

"Sorry, Marge. This is Hayley Alexander and her baby girl, Christine. Hayley, meet my sister, Marge."

"Alexander. Where have I heard that name before?" Marge queried, perplexed. Christine reached out for Hayley, and Marge handed her over.

Looking vaguely uncomfortable, Dillon insinuated himself between the two women. "I don't know. There are plenty of Alexanders around. Alexander Haig. Alexander the Great. There's even a St. Alexander—''

Marge aimed a punch at Dillon's sternum. "Cut it out. You know what I mean." She pivoted back to Hayley. "I'm serious. Have we met?"

"No, I don't think so. I just met Dillon yesterday when we first talked about the job," Hayley said. "Unless he mentioned to you that he had hired me as his new housekeeper."

"Hayley is your new housekeeper?"

Dillon nodded. "Close your jaw, Marge, or Hayley will be insulted."

Marge made a face at him, then turned back to Hayley. "Sorry, Hayley, no offense. But I thought Dillon was going to hire someone much older and—uh—settled. You know, someone with the efficiency of a Marine." Catching her brother's dark warning look, she amended with an elegant little shrug, "Guess not."

"As it happens, Hayley is very efficient," Dillon put in.

How would he know? Hayley wondered, very much aware she hadn't yet been given a chance to prove herself.

"Did I say she wasn't?" Marge countered.

"She even knows how to replace the washers in a faucet."

"That's good, because you sure don't." Marge grinned. She turned back to Hayley. "I'm sorry I was so surprised. I thought—by the way you were dressed and everything—that you were Dillon's friend."

*Meaning "lady friend,"* Hayley thought, uncomfortably embarrassed. Was this a conclusion everyone else would make, too? Would she constantly be explaining to everyone they weren't lovers? Piqued she hadn't thought about that before, she looked at Dillon. "Did you want me to wear a uniform?" she asked.

"No, of course not." Dillon's glance slid approvingly over her shawl-collar menswear jacket, red shell and black stirrup pants. "You can dress any way you want."

Marge nodded vigorously. "I agree. There is absolutely no reason why Hayley should have to a wear a uniform. Not in this day and age."

Christine squirmed and Hayley put her down. As the three of them talked some more about the strengths and weaknesses of Dillon's new house, they watched Christine crawling about, exploring the sprawling first floor.

While Dillon went into the utility room off the large country kitchen to check out the fuse box, Hayley observed Marge's rapt gaze. "You really like babies, don't you?"

"Oh, yes," Marge admitted with a yearning smile. "Even more so, now that my own children are out of the nest."

Dillon rejoined them, adding, "To the point, she's doing everything she can to get me to procreate one for her to fuss over."

"Well, Dillon," Marge delivered a heartfelt sigh, "you are forty—"

Dillon narrowed his eyes at her. "Don't you have a nursery school class to teach today?"

"Nope. I'm all done for the day. I'm through at noon, remember?"

Dillon groaned.

Marge knelt down to explore a red satin throw pillow with black fringe with Christine. "Now that my three kids are off at college, I'd do anything to have a baby in my life again." She looked at Hayley, woman-to-woman.

"You're very lucky to have such an adorable child. Enjoy these days while they last."

Hayley thought of the year ahead of her, and even though she knew it would be fraught with hard work, she anticipated only happiness. "I intend to," she said.

"I APOLOGIZE for my sister," Dillon said the moment Marge left; Christine napped peacefully in the playpen Hayley had brought with her.

Hayley paused to lift two paintings off the living room wall. "I thought she was very nice."

Dillon took the paintings from her and put them in the trash. "And hopelessly outspoken," he continued.

"That, too," Hayley remarked, inhaling the bracing scent of his cologne as he came back to her side. "But it's very clear she loves you and wants only the best for you. I envy you that."

He gave her a searching look, the intensity of his regard drawing her eyes to the rugged lines of his face. "You don't have any brothers and sisters?" he asked in a soft, low voice.

"No." Aware that she was having trouble catching her breath standing so near to him, and that it was ridiculous for her to be reacting that way, Hayley stepped back. Picking up a ficus plant that was deader than a doornail, she carried it to the trash. "Though maybe I should be glad about that," she teased over her shoulder, "considering how anxious yours is to marry you off."

Dillon strode after her, each of his long, easy strides matching her two. "Don't remind me," he groaned, keeping his voice low, so as not to wake the baby. "Not that it's anything new. Marge has been trying to fix me up with the right woman ever since I can remember."

"Without much luck, obviously," Hayley observed.

"Every time I come home she's got at least one potential mate waiting in the wings."

"And?" Hayley picked up a telephone shaped like the head of Daffy Duck and held it up for his perusal.

"And I don't believe in fairy tales," Dillon said, unhooking the phone from the wall and placing it atop the pile marked for charity.

"Neither do I," she admitted.

"Unfortunately most women do," Dillon continued gruffly. "And I'm no knight on a white charger."

Their gazes met, held. For a moment Hayley felt she could drown in the dark blue depths of his eyes. To her surprise, he looked similarly entranced. This job was going to be both easier and harder than she'd thought.

"So, which master suite do you want?" he asked, finally recovering enough to break their staring match. "The one at the top of the stairs, or the one at the far end of the hall, over the garage?"

"The one nearest the stairs, so I can get up with the baby at night.

"Fine with me. What about the furniture?" Dillon continued, leading the way up the stairs and into the master suite that would be Hayley's.

Hayley looked around at the sunny yellow walls and thought it had possibilities. If only this were going to be her house, too, and not just Dillon's, she thought wistfully, aware she was already falling in love with the place, envisioning the way it could and would be. "I'd like to bring my own, if it's okay. Except for the brass bed. It's really nice. Unless you have other plans for it—"

"Not a one." Dillon shot her a wicked grin, as if the mention of a bed, any bed, brought all sorts of thoughts to mind. But then, to her relief, he merely shrugged his broad shoulders laconically.

Hayley fought a blush and averted her eyes. "Then I'd like to use the frame." Hayley lovingly ran her palm across the curved top of the bedstead. "I always wanted a brass bed," she confessed. "That or an old-fashioned canopy bed." She'd always thought them so romantic. Funny that she would be getting one now, when there wasn't so much as a chance for romance in her life. And yet, she thought wistfully, it would be so easy for her to imagine her and a lover in that bed. A lover as sexy as Dillon.

"You didn't have one when you were a kid?" Dillon watched her methodically strip the bedspread and the sheets.

"No," Hayley said quietly, irritated with the direction of her thoughts. She knew better than to fantasize like that about an employer. Thankful Dillon couldn't read her mind, she continued, "I didn't." But she didn't want to think about that. Her childhood years had been rough enough without dwelling on them.

Dillon circled around to the opposite side of the bed. The corners of his sensual mouth pulled down into a frown. "The mattress and box springs are in terrible shape. Look. You can even see the coils sticking through."

"I'll bring my own," Hayley said, absently, still pre-occupied and faintly disturbed by the unusually erotic line of her thoughts.

His frown deepened. "The frame looks a little tarnished."

"I can fix that easily enough," Hayley said confidently. "All it will take is a little polish."

What wouldn't be so easy to fix, she thought, was her continued physical reaction to Dillon. Every time he got within three feet of her, her heart sped up. Her breathing became more shallow. Her palms started sweating. And her thoughts...her thoughts!

She wanted this job and wanted it badly. It was perfect for her and her baby. But could she live with the tension she was feeling now for the whole next year? She supposed, as she tried as unobtrusively as possible to blot her hands on the wool gabardine of her blazer, she would have to.

DILLON HEARD the tap-tap-tap the moment he walked in the door. He followed the noise to the kitchen. Hayley was on her hands and knees. She had a hammer in one hand, a chisel in the other. She was clad in sapphire blue stretch pants, a matching tank top and a striped man's shirt, worn open to the waist. High-top white and blue running shoes were laced tightly up over her trim ankles. He stared at her raised bottom and slender thighs incredulously, unwilling to admit to himself what the sight of her, stretched out that way, did to him. She was his housekeeper, he reminded himself firmly. And she had been for the past two incredibly long weeks.

He had no business thinking of her in this way. No business imagining what her thick and wavy honey blond hair, which was caught up in a youthful ponytail on top of her head, would look like if it were down, falling gloriously around her slender shoulders. Or how she would react if he gave in to his baser impulses and knelt down on the floor beside her, took her in his arms and kissed her senseless.

He wasn't lord of the manor. These weren't feudal times.

Before he had a chance to speak, a floor tile went sailing past him, into the trash.

"Hi, Dillon," Hayley said, without missing a beat.

"Where's Christine?"

"Asleep for the night in her crib." Hayley pointed to the baby monitor on the counter; it was blissfully silent. Tap-tap-tap. She was already working on the next tile.

Dillon forced his eyes away from her and stared at the exposed cement floor with its gobs of old dried glue. "I thought my house looked like hell *before* you got started," he said dryly.

Hayley sat up breathlessly. Her face was flushed, her chest heaving with exertion. "Very funny."

"What the devil are you doing? Or shouldn't I ask?" It looked as if she was a one-woman demolition crew, busy tearing the hell out of his kitchen. Not to mention the rest of the house, which looked worse, day by day.

"I'm taking up the tile," Hayley answered him, exasperated. "What does it look like?"

"If I knew I wouldn't have asked."

Hayley wrapped her arms around her bent knees. "It's easy enough to do."

Dillon knelt beside her. His gaze roved her mussed hair and bright green eyes. Damn, but she looked beautiful tonight. "Do you have any idea how late it is?"

"Midnight or a little after. Why?" Hayley stripped off her rubber gloves and laid them on a dry patch of floor beside her. She sat with her back against the cabinets, one leg stretched out flat, the other bent at the knee.

"Where'd you learn to do this?"

"One of my uncles was a construction worker whose firm specialized in remodeling jobs. I spent a summer as his apprentice."

"That's how you know plumbing, too, I guess."

"No. I learned plumbing from one of my cousins when I was in high school. His dad was a plumber. The two of us used to assist him on jobs, both for the knowledge—

plumbing's a handy thing to know—and for spending money.''

''I see.'' He wished like hell her tank top were cut just a tad higher, so he couldn't see the shadowy cleft between her breasts. And he wished her matching pants were a tad looser. They hugged her cute body and sensually outlined her long lissome thighs and curvaceous calves.

''I suppose you want dinner,'' Hayley guessed.

Dillon leaned against the kitchen counter and told himself it wasn't her beauty that kept him from firing her on the spot but his faith that she would eventually make some sort of order out of all this chaos, chaos that seemed to get worse every day. ''Is there any?'' he asked hopefully, aware just how hungry he was, and that there was a disturbing lack of homey cooking smells in the kitchen.

Hayley shrugged. ''Not unless you count the leftover broccoli from last night.''

Dillon's hopes of a hot, hearty meal faded fast. He knew he should have grabbed something from the machines at work. Or ordered in. Now, because he was living in the suburbs where everything closed down much earlier, it was too late.

He climbed over her and headed for the refrigerator. Hayley was not turning out to be much of a housekeeper. She never had any food fixed for him. And though his clothes were usually clean, they were never ironed. ''You know I thought the house would be taking shape by now. Instead it just seems to be getting more torn up.''

''All the remodeling getting to you, huh?'' She grinned and bounced up off the floor. ''Thought so. Well, I've got a surprise for you. You'll never guess what came today!''

''The water heater guy?'' he guessed hopefully.

''No, sorry,'' she said, her eyes fastening for a moment on the scar that ran from his wrist to his elbow and was visible beneath the rolled-up sleeves of his navy blue shirt. "The plumber can't get here until tomorrow. But we're still getting enough hot water to take a shower, so don't worry."

Dillon didn't deny that the excess of cold water had done him some good the past few days. He never should have told her she could dress however she wanted. Of course, how was he to know that she'd look sexy as hell in literally everything she chose to wear? "How long a shower?"

"Five minutes, maybe."

"And how long before you can take another?"

"Hard to say. At least an hour. Probably a little more. It depends on how hot you like the water."

*Or your women. Now where had that thought come from?* Struggling to keep his mind on the conversation, he wiped a bead of perspiration from his upper lip and said, "I'm surprised you're not more frustrated." He sure as hell would've been. He hadn't nearly the patience of Hayley, who was more and more beginning to look like a saint. Or even worse in his estimation—a born suburbanite.

"It's been fun, getting started on the house," she said with a reassuring smile. "Which brings us back to what I was trying to tell you a few minutes ago. Your furniture from Riyadh arrived today. I had the movers put it in the study." She started off in that direction and inclined her head, willing him to follow.

Dillon followed her through the formal dining room, into the hall, and then to the study at the rear of the house. He couldn't believe she had done so much in so little time. Boxes of books had yet to be placed into the built-in shelves on either side of the stone fireplace, but the cherry colored leather sofa and matching armchairs, his desk, lamps, and end tables had been arranged. A Persian rug had been rolled out over the slate gray carpet in the paneled room. The only thing missing was suitable drapes for the windows. He looked around, feeling remarkably content, even if he, a confirmed city dweller, was now living in suburbia. "This is really great," Dillon said.

"I figured you needed one room in the house where you could relax. Though I eventually intend to tackle this from the bottom up, too."

Dillon was barely able to stifle a groan. He could only imagine what havoc she'd wreak in here when she got ready.

Briefly her white teeth scraped across her lower lip. "But in the meantime, it'll stay as is, your haven against the ongoing remodeling in the rest of the house. Is the furniture how you wanted it?"

"Exactly how I wanted it," Dillon said, marveling once again at her ability to read his mind. But it wouldn't do to get too cozy with her. He was helping her back on her feet. Doing what he owed Hank, and that was all.

THREE AFTERNOONS LATER the doorbell rang. Thinking it another delivery man with a slew of boxes for Dillon from Riyadh or some other far-off place, Hayley put down her chisel and hammer and headed for the front door.

"Welcome to the neighborhood!" Two women in tennis outfits held out Tupperware containers.

"We would have dropped by sooner, but we wanted to give you a couple of weeks to get settled. I'm Carol," a pleasant-looking woman with short brown hair began, warmly shaking Hayley's hand. "I brought chocolate brownies. And this is Nellie. She brought you her special honey and oatmeal bread."

"Thank you," Hayley said, surprised and pleased. She

wanted to get to know the other people in the neighborhood. Maybe when she did, there would be other children for Christine to play with. A mother's club for her to join, a play group for Christine... "This is awfully nice of you." Although she wanted to invite the women in, she paused uncertainly, not sure how Dillon would feel about her entertaining neighborhood guests.

"Everything is all right over here, isn't it?" Nellie asked. "I couldn't help but notice your husband didn't take the train in this morning with everyone else."

Hayley wasn't sure whether she was piqued or amused by Nellie's nosiness. She just knew her situation was unusual. Would they shun her and Christine if they realized she was really hired help? Or would they continue to treat her in the same warm, welcoming manner?

"Everything's fine," Hayley said, forcing herself to put her worries aside and smile politely. "Dillon's just catching up on his sleep. He had to work most of last night, monitoring a breaking story."

"Dillon, he would be your husband?" Nellie asked.

"Uh, boss, actually," Hayley corrected. "I'm his housekeeper."

"Oh," Carol said, looking stunned; then she smiled. "That's wonderful."

Hayley smiled back, blessing Carol for her open-mindedness.

"And Mrs. Gallagher?" Nellie asked point blank, her smile seeming more nosy than sincere. "Is she here today?"

Hayley took a deep breath. Maybe she was a fool, but until now she hadn't considered how the other people in the neighborhood would react to her living here with Dillon, without a "Mrs." on the premises. "There is no Mrs.

Gallagher,'' she retorted frankly. "Dillon's not married. And neither am I.''

"I see,'' Nellie said heavily.

Hayley doubted that, but she wasn't in the habit of telling her life story to every stranger she met on the street, and she wasn't about to start now. Carol, on the other hand, was someone she could see herself becoming quite good friends with. "Well, if you'll excuse me,'' she began politely, "I really do need to get back to work. I've got so much to do, getting this place into shape, that I can't afford to waste my baby's nap time.''

"We understand,'' Carol put in before Nellie could speak. "But before you go, there is one more thing. We'd like to invite you to a barbecue at my home, Saturday evening. It's a get-together for all the neighbors. It'd be a good chance for you and Dillon to meet everyone. And of course children are welcome so you can bring your baby.''

Hayley wasn't up on suburban etiquette, but she was fairly certain that most of the residents didn't bring their hired help to parties. On the other hand she was going to be living here, too, for the next year. And so would Christine. She wanted to make friends with the people in the neighborhood. She hoped Dillon would, too, but even if he didn't, that wasn't going to stop her, no more than his distaste for suburbia would stop her from settling here in Connecticut permanently.

"I'll tell Dillon about the invitation and ask him if he'd like to come,'' she promised. "I'll definitely be there.''

"I THOUGHT I HEARD the doorbell,'' Dillon said several hours later. He strode into the kitchen and paused to probe her eyes.

In a khaki shirt worn open at the throat, faded jeans

that fit his lower body like a glove and hiking boots that had definitely seen better days, he looked casual and at ease. His dark brown hair was agreeably tousled, his jaw clean shaven and scented with after-shave. His dark blue eyes were alive with interest.

"You certainly did," Hayley finally confirmed. She couldn't believe how good Dillon looked. And on so little sleep...

"What the—" For the first time, Dillon noticed what Hayley had been dealing with for several hours. He stared at the confections, casseroles, salads and breads that lined the kitchen counters and covered the breakfast nook table. "Where did all this come from?" he asked, amazed.

Hayley straightened and shut the refrigerator door. She leaned back against it. "Would you believe almost half of our, uh, neighbors stopped by to say hello?"

Dillon quirked a dark, disbelieving brow. "All at once?"

Hayley tossed him a wry smile. "It seems they noticed you didn't take the train in to New York this morning. It also seems that they're drowning in curiosity about us."

Dillon pulled up a kitchen chair, turned it around backward and slid into it, folding his arms over the back. His eyes glimmered with suppressed amusement. "What'd you tell them?"

"Not nearly as much as they'd like." Hayley grinned back impudently.

"Bet they're frustrated as hell," Dillon predicted.

"And running out of Tupperware containers," Hayley said, trying hard not to notice how rock hard his thighs looked beneath the soft, much-washed fabric of his jeans as he straddled the chair. She forced her gaze back to the rugged contours of his face. "There's more. One of the women, Carol, and her husband, Hal, are throwing a barbecue Saturday night. They've invited all three of us. I've already promised to attend with Christine. You're welcome to go over with us. But if you'd rather go alone," she went on hurriedly, "you know, arrive separately, I understand."

Dillon almost choked. "Are you kidding? I'd sooner have my teeth drilled than attend some suburban get-to-know-you bash."

Hayley had half suspected he might react that way.

"Never mind about going it *alone*," Dillon muttered. "No, if we're going, and we probably should for the sake of neighborhood harmony, we're going together."

"Are you sure?" she asked, thinking maybe it would seem too much like a date. She was already fantasizing about him as it was and about what it would be like to live here permanently. "It might seem a little odd to people for you to take your housekeeper and her child along to a party," she managed.

He quirked a brow.

"I mean, wouldn't it cramp your style if…we were together?"

Dillon grinned. "First of all, I doubt there's anyone I want to date at this party. Second, nothing cramps my style, I assure you. If I want to go after a woman, I go after her all the way. I don't care who's watching. Third, you're not getting out of this. It's just as important for you to meet everyone out here as it is for me. After all, you're probably going to be around more. And you never know when you'll need a helping hand."

*True,* Hayley thought.

"Or want to be available to lend one to someone else," Dillon continued. He tested one of Carol's frosted walnut brownies. "And even if it is dull, it can't last all that long. Besides—" he grinned at Christine, who was in her high chair "—we can always use your little darling as an excuse to leave early."

## Chapter Three

"Tell the truth, Dillon. Hayley's not really your house-keeper, is she?" Bob asked, casting a lustful glance in Hayley's direction. "You guys are shacking up together. Aren't you?"

Dillon sampled a Mexican meatball and decided to play dumb. "You mean living under the same roof?" he asked, wondering for the thousandth time why he'd come to the backyard social. Not that he minded the company or the food; he just wasn't used to having the details of his private life open to public discussion. Hayley had been right. They *were* the talk of the entire neighborhood.

"I mean making whoopee," Bob corrected. "You know. The ultimate act."

Dillon wondered if he could be convicted for his thoughts. In his thoughts he and Hayley had made love plenty of times.

Hal left the grill to join the group of men sampling the array of hors d'oeuvres. "What's the powwow about, guys?"

"We were just talking about Dillon's housekeeper," Bob confided with a look behind him to make sure none of the women—most of whom were busy in Carol's kitchen—was within earshot. "I personally find it hard to believe that Hayley is just Dillon's housekeeper."

"What gives you guys the idea I'd want a live-in mistress?" Dillon challenged them all casually. He'd always shied away from that. Too many complications. Too much potential for domestic hassles, none of which he found attractive.

"Come on!" Bob said. "A gorgeous woman like that! Who wouldn't want to go to bed with her!"

*True,* Dillon thought. Hayley was a constant temptation. Everything she wore, everything she did or said, no matter how subtle or ordinary, prompted endless yearning and fantasizing on his part.

"Sounds like she's angling for more than a housekeeping job to me," Bob remarked, helping himself to another beer from the washtub full of ice. "Sounds like she's auditioning for a position as your wife."

Chuck grinned at Bob. "You only wish your wife looked like that. Who cares if she doesn't cook?"

"Dillon sure doesn't!" All the guys laughed.

Turning back to Dillon, Bob remarked, "Sorry if I've been ribbing you. I guess I'm just envious of the setup you've got. A gorgeous young woman to take care of you and see to your every need without the complications of marriage."

The only problem was, Dillon thought, she wasn't seeing to his every need. Even if she was fueling his every fantasy.

"What you've got going for you, Dillon," Bob continued, "is every guy's fantasy."

"Yeah, I've got it made all right," Dillon said. He had no outlet for his passion. And yet he knew instinctively, even if Hayley didn't, how great it would be if the two of them ever did get together.

"Not necessarily," Hal disagreed. "I mean, she could fall in love with somebody else and pack up and leave Dillon at any time, so there's no security in that."

"True," Chuck agreed.

The idea of Hayley packing up and walking out on him made Dillon's throat burn more than the cayenne pepper in the Mexican meatballs. "I don't think so," Dillon disagreed shortly.

Everyone turned to look at him. He shifted uncomfortably. "She was really in love with Hank," he defended her objectively. "I don't think she's looking to replace him with anyone else."

"Maybe not," Hal sighed. "But face it. Guys are going to be hitting on her night and day, once word gets out that she's single and you're not making any permanent claim on her. The only reason the single guys in the community haven't already approached her is everyone thought—well, it looked like—we just assumed the two of you were married or at least—"

"Cohabitating," Chuck supplied tactfully.

Dillon sent his brother-in-law a dark look.

Chuck shrugged. "Sorry, Dillon. You know I don't mean anything by it but the guys are right. Hayley is gorgeous and you've got a heck of a reputation as a ladies' man. Of course, now everyone knows you've got no intention of marrying her, the guys are going to be lining up at your door, trying to get her to go out with them."

Just the thought of Hayley going out with someone else made Dillon's gut tighten. "Wait a minute," he interrupted. "I never said she was up for grabs."

"Aha! I told you guys! They are—"

"What I mean is, she's got a lot left to do on the house," Dillon managed. A whole year's worth. And in a whole year, who knew what might happen between them? "Decorating, unpacking, overseeing repairs."

"Yeah, Nellie told me she'd torn holy hell out of that house," Bob sympathized.

And she had yet to begin to put it back together again, Dillon thought. Except for his den and both their bedrooms, the place was a wreck.

"Even so, she must have some time off," Hal said.

"Why not fix her up if you're not interested?" Chuck asked. "A woman that nice shouldn't be alone."

Dillon turned to his brother-in-law and stifled the urge to shoot him. "You're a big help, Chuck," he said dryly. "And the reason I'm not fixing her up is 'cause she's still vulnerable."

"She doesn't look that vulnerable to me. In fact, she doesn't seem to be grieving much at all," Hal said thoughtfully.

"Why should she be, when she's got Dillon to keep her warm nights?" Bob joked.

The backyard echoed with raucous male laughter.

"Admit it, Dillon," Bob continued, slapping him on the back, "you've got it made in the shade!"

"HOW COULD YOU have done that to me?" Hayley demanded, the moment they'd returned to the house and she'd put Christine to bed.

Baffled by her obvious pique with him, Dillon followed her down the upstairs hall to her bedroom. "Done what?"

Hayley planted both hands on her hips and whirled to face him. "Marge's husband told her verbatim what you men were laughing and talking about with such hilarity just before dinner."

Dillon uttered a string of swear words as he recalled all the bad jokes that had been made. Worse, he'd reveled in the fact he was the envy of every man there. "I don't get it," he said to no one in particular. "Why would she do something like that?"

"Why would *she* do something like that? What about *you?* Besides, she wanted to know what everyone else there wanted to know!" Bright spots of color appeared in Hayley's cheeks.

"Which is?"

"If we're sleeping together!"

Dillon watched as Hayley hauled a suitcase off the shelf in her closet, marched to the bed and flung it open. "I told the guys we weren't," he said flatly.

"With a glint in your eye and a smile on your face!"

"So sue me for laughing at those guys! It was funny!" Dillon defended himself hotly. Hayley knew how conventional the residents of this suburban Connecticut community were. Hell, he had even joked about it before they went to the party.

"Well, I'm not laughing," she informed him between tightly gritted teeth. Hayley stalked to her dresser drawer and pulled out a handful of some of the most filmy, lacy lingerie Dillon had ever seen in his life. Shoulders back, she flung her hair out of her face.

Dillon bit down on a string of curse words. It was too late to take back all the kidding around that he'd done. The most he could do was manage a save. And, judging from the thundercloud looks she was giving him, that looked like it was going to be one hell of a task. "Hayley, come on," he coaxed softly, stepping as near to her bed as he dared. "Be reasonable here. I said I'm sorry."

She whirled on him. For a moment he thought she was going to try to deck him. Instead she planted her balled-up fists on her slender hips. "Sorry doesn't cut it here, Dillon. We had one chance to be accepted in this neigh-

borhood. One. And you blew it with your macho antics."
She'd hoped, foolishly it now seemed, they could be
friends. Even more than friends.

But she'd been wrong. Otherwise Dillon never
would've joked with the other men about her. Worse, he
had blown her chance to be really accepted by the women
in the community. She didn't want to lose her dream,
especially when it had all seemed just within her grasp.
But she would if this was the way Dillon intended to act,
and apparently he did.

Dillon sobered. He ran a hand across his jaw and realized that although he'd used a razor before the party, he
needed another shave. "I'll set them all straight," he
promised. He didn't want to lose Hayley. Didn't want her
to bail out on him before he'd had a chance to somehow
do right by Hank and see that his widow and infant child
were not just surviving all right, but were well situated
for their future. Not to mention the fact that for the first
time in his life he looked forward to coming home at
night.

"It doesn't matter what you say now, Dillon. They
won't believe you. After what you intimated tonight, the
only way our relationship could be legitimized in their
eyes is if we were to admit everyone else was right about
us all along and marry."

"So marry me," he said.

Her eyes were liquid pools of pure dark green. "That
isn't funny, either," she said.

Dillon felt even more guilty. He'd never meant to hurt
her. "Who's being funny?" he said softly, trying once
again to approach her, his hands outstretched. "I don't
want you to leave." Damn it, he liked having her here,
even if she did turn his house and his life upside down.

She elbowed him aside and strode militantly toward her

closet again. "Well, isn't that just too bad!" She pulled out a handful of negligees, hangers and all. Dillon was disconcerted to see those were even sexier than her undergarments.

His mouth dry, he paced toward her beseechingly, then followed her back toward her suitcase. This was no time to be thinking about what a great body she had or how incredibly enticing she'd look in those filmy garments. "You can't leave me with this mess."

She folded the negligees and placed them neatly in her suitcase. "Just watch me."

Dillon tore his eyes from a lace gown and thought about all the tiles she had ripped up, the light fixtures she'd torn out, the cabinets that had been sanded to bare wood. "I'll never be able to finish."

"So what?" Was she supposed to care about that? When she had just lost the one and only chance she'd ever had to *live* her dream, even for a little while?

"So there goes your share of the profits," Dillon pointed out smugly. Her face fell. But only for a minute.

"So I'll come in days while you're gone and finish," she shot back triumphantly.

Dillon crossed his arms over his chest. He stood, legs braced apart. He hadn't expected her to be so damn stubborn. "And live where in the meantime?" he asked. Because he knew it would irritate her, he let his eyes trail slowly over her honey blond hair before returning with laser accuracy to her thick-lashed green eyes. "You already sublet your apartment in the city, remember?"

Hayley's chin shot up another notch. "You think I'm backed into a corner financially, do you?"

Dillon smiled and twisted the knife in a little deeper. She wasn't the only one who could threaten with impending disaster. "You *know* you are, sweetheart."

"You did this on purpose."

"Yeah, sure I did," he agreed. "I went to that party tonight determined to start a fight with you that would force you to leave my employ. I want my house to look like a nuclear disaster. I want to lose my entire life savings over this."

"Well, maybe you didn't want it, but you sure got us into this mess, and now we're stuck with it," she said, looking equally distressed with herself and with him.

Her chest rose and fell with each furious breath. Color flooded her cheeks. Her eyes glittered. Her sensual lips pursed. She had never looked more beautiful to Dillon, or more inaccessible. He had never wanted to kiss her more. Suddenly he knew he couldn't let her go. Not like this, anyway. Unfortunately she was right; there was only one way she could stay and retain any shred of reputation there.

But damn it all, he didn't *want* to get married. Didn't *want* to fall into some dull domestic trap. On the other hand, who said they had to do things the usual way? God knew they hadn't so far. "Look, Hayley," he said impatiently. "You know what the solution to this is. We have to—" he choked out the words in a strangled voice "—get married. But don't worry," he soothed. "It'll be purely a business arrangement."

"You really are an egotistical jerk, aren't you?" Hayley tossed her mane of golden hair and sent him a withering look. "For your information, Dillon Gallagher, I wouldn't marry you if you were the last man on earth."

She meant it. Desperate not to be left alone to deal with the rubble the interior of his house was in, he searched for a way to keep her. He had already offered her ten percent of the sale profits. "Okay, okay," he said frantically, as she closed the first suitcase and glided regally to the closet to pull out another. "I'll up the ante. I'll give you thirty percent of the profits from the sale." Surely, he thought confidently, she couldn't turn that down! Not when he desperately needed her to stay.

She stared at him with a hauteur that would have turned a lesser man to ice. He knew then she'd stop at nothing to make him pay for what he'd done to her. "Fifty percent of the profits," she demanded in a cool, calculated tone, "and you've got a deal." Her soft pink lips formed in a brittle smile. "One penny less and I walk!"

"That's highway robbery!" Dillon exclaimed.

"You're catching on," she said.

Dillon's jaw set. "That's way too much money!" he volleyed back.

She lifted her delicate shoulders in a careless shrug. "Considering all you've asked me to do here, Dillon, I don't think so. Besides," her voice turned practical again, "we'll easily get double the money you paid for the place when I'm done with it, if we bide our time during the sale and pick the right realtor. Marge was right, you got this place at a steal."

Dillon was silent. "All right," he said finally. "Because you've already ripped the house to shreds and I'd lose more money if I had to hire someone else at this point, I'll—" He choked. For a moment he was unable to go on. "I'll give you fifty percent," he finished irritably.

Hayley's face lit up. "Great." She turned away from him and methodically opened up the second suitcase she'd laid across the bed. "I'm still moving out first thing tomorrow, but I'll—"

"Moving where?" He was vaguely aware he was beginning to panic all over again. His insides twisted into a pretzellike knot.

"I don't know." Hayley made another beeline for the dresser. This time she returned with a stack of workout clothes and leotards. She placed them neatly in one corner of the suitcase, then pivoted back for another handful. "Your sister Marge and I get along well. Perhaps she'll let Christine and me stay there temporarily and pay rent. Her kids are off at college and she has extra space."

Being humiliated in the neighborhood, by having Hayley walk out on him, was one thing. Having his sister not only in on the mess he'd made, but cleaning up after him, was quite another. "You can't do that," he said. By God, if she was going to get fifty percent of the profits from the house out of this, then he was going to get something out of it, too. He wanted their budding friendship back.

"After what you did to me tonight, I have no choice."

"I told you. I'll straighten it out."

She sent him an exasperated look. "I only wish it were that simple, Dillon, but you know as well as I that once a woman is considered involved with a man that's a hard assumption to shake off, particularly in a conservative neighborhood like this. I have Christine to consider. I want to reside in Connecticut permanently. I don't want this assumption about us coming back to haunt me years from now. I have an example to set for Christine."

"Don't you think you're overreacting a bit?"

"Maybe. I don't know. I only know I'm upset by this. If I'm upset by gossip, I expect she will be, too."

"Then I'll marry you," he repeated sternly.

Hayley scowled at him. "I told you before I didn't think that was funny."

Dillon slid his hands into his back pockets. He just didn't want her to leave. "Who's joking?" Dillon asked calmly.

"Dillon—"

"We could make it work, Hayley. Just until you finish the house and we sell it, you understand. Then we'll get an annulment. In the meantime, we could go on as we have been." It made perfect sense.

"You make it sound so simple," she said, sighing.

Dillon shrugged and said, "It would be, as long as no one else but us knew it was just a business arrangement."

Her eyes widened. "You want everyone to think it's a real marriage?"

"I think that would be best, yes."

Hayley swallowed and backed away from him uncomfortably. "I don't like subterfuge, Dillon."

He watched her sit down on the edge of the bed, beside her open suitcase. As she began to relax, so did he. "Neither do I but sometimes it's the only way, and in this case I know I'm right. If Marge knew, she'd try to talk me out of it. She'd say it was a crazy thing to do."

Hayley was back on her feet again in a flash, moving restlessly about the room. "She might be right."

He watched the color climb her cheeks again and couldn't help but grin, she was so edgy and unnerved. "Not adult enough to handle it?" he taunted lightly.

She shot him a sharp look, meant to debilitate, but all it did was intrigue him. What was she so wary of?

"What's the matter, Hayley?" he continued, teasing her gently, yet wanting, needing, to see her reaction all the same. "Don't you think you could live under the same roof with me and not sleep with me?"

Hayley crossed her arms at her waist. "Don't flatter yourself."

"See?" Dillon said, as even more fire came into her eyes, making her look simultaneously sexy and unapproachable as hell. "We're acting like an old married couple already. Sniping. Trading barbs." He grinned at her unrepentantly.

Slowly, her sense of humor returned. She smiled back at him, just as audaciously. "This is crazy," she repeated, in a low voice that let him know she was almost sold on the idea.

"It'll work," Dillon promised.

Without warning, Hayley's brow furrowed. "What'll we do?"

"About what?"

Hayley gulped again. "About sex."

*Now they were talking,* Dillon thought, his mind going back to that sexy lingerie and the unbearably sexy way he imagined she would look in it. "Hey, if you want to write that in, too…" he offered magnanimously.

"No," Hayley said swiftly, her color heightening even more.

"Too bad. I was looking forward to—"

She whirled toward him. "These are not feudal times, Dillon Gallagher. You may not exercise that right, even if we do make it legal. Understood?"

"Understood," he repeated obediently. It wouldn't keep him from making love to her, though, if and when the time and the mood were ever just right. And he had a whole year to try and see that they were.

"And if either one of us wants to be with someone else," Hayley continued in a strangled voice as she avoided his laser-bright gaze, "we can do so, as long as we're discreet."

Dillon didn't like the idea of Hayley with anyone else, but he also knew he had no right to protest. "Agreed." he said, assuring himself silently that Hayley was just talking big to save face. He believed the truth was that she was just as attracted to him as he was to her, even if she hadn't allowed herself to act on that attraction yet.

"So when do you want to do this thing?" she asked.

Dillon tried not to look too happy. "You're saying yes?"

Hayley looked at him, her expression unaccountably grim. She uttered a lengthy sigh. "What other choice do I have?"

# Chapter Four

"I finally remembered who she is, Dillon," Marge said, early the following Thursday afternoon. She held a copy of the Darien News in her hands. The marriage licenses section was circled in red. "I remembered why the name Alexander was so familiar to me. Hayley's husband Hank was one of the NCN reporters killed while covering Desert Storm, wasn't he? He was one of your reporters."

Dillon shut the door connecting his private office to the newsroom. In the silence that fell, he could hear his heart thudding heavily in his chest. "Have you said anything about this to anyone?" he demanded.

Marge blinked. "I told Chuck—"

"Besides your husband," Dillon qualified irritably.

"No." Marge glared at him.

He glared back. "Well don't. Okay?"

Marge's dark blue eyes narrowed. "Hayley doesn't know, does she?" Marge guessed. "You never told her you were the one responsible for her husband's death."

Dillon sat forward. His mood was suddenly as grim as his low voice. "I had no way of knowing the army barracks would be hit when I sent Hank on that assignment. It was a routine jaunt. Safer than almost anything over there."

"I'm sorry, Dillon. I didn't mean to imply you were responsible. But I know how you felt after Hank Alexander's death. I remember the letters you wrote—"

"I meant to tell her. I tried."

"Why didn't you?"

"Because when I first went to see her, she didn't want to hear it. So I let it go." He'd felt all the worse because Hayley had told him how much Hank had respected him as a boss.

"But things are different now, Dillon."

"Are they? Hayley still wants to get on with her life."

"She should know."

"When the time is right," Dillon qualified.

"And when will that be?"

"I expect I'll know when it happens."

"Are you sure you're doing the right thing?"

"No." Dillon swallowed. "I wish Hank hadn't been killed and Hayley left a widow. But she was. And I'm dealing with it as best I can." Although he still didn't know what he wanted from her in the long run. Forgiveness? Maybe. A love affair? Definitely. Beyond that, he just didn't know.

For the next few seconds, both he and his sister were extraordinarily quiet. She covered his hand with her own. "I'm not blaming you, Dillon," she said gently. "And I don't think Hayley would, either, once all the facts were out. I do think Hayley should be told the truth before you marry her. For heaven's sake, Dillon, she has a right to know!"

"No." Dillon turned away from his sister. The situation had already snowballed into something unpleasant. He didn't want to risk a new avalanche of damage. He didn't want to risk losing her, not as his housekeeper, not as his potential lover.

"Why not?" Marge insisted.

"Because it's over, that's why not." He paced back and forth. "Because talking about it would upset her."

"You're making a mistake," Marge warned.

"It's mine to make," Dillon volleyed back stubbornly.

Marge studied him, her disappointment obvious. "I can't talk you out of it?"

"The only thing you'll be talked out of if you keep this up," Dillon retorted, "is your invitation to my wedding on Saturday."

Marge reached blindly for a chair and sank into it weakly. "You're doing it that soon?"

Dillon shrugged. He'd been debating all week whether or not to tell his sister that this marriage was going to be a purely business arrangement between himself and Hayley. Now, seeing how distraught she was over the little she knew, he was glad he hadn't. "Neither of us sees any reason to wait." What he did with his life was his business, he assured himself sternly.

Marge let out a slow, unsteady breath. "Under the circumstances, I don't think you should be marrying her at all, and certainly not yet."

"That's funny." Dillon propped his feet on his desk. He regarded his sister with unchecked pique. "I don't recall asking your advice."

"I know." Marge smiled at him with sisterly concern. As usual when they disagreed about the mess she felt he was making with his life, she refused to back off. "It's free, anyway. At the very least, do it right," Marge urged with a smile. "Have a proper engagement and honeymoon, a big wedding with all your family and friends."

Dillon shook his head, nixing that idea at once. "We don't want to wait."

"I thought Hayley was practical."

"She is." Dillon smiled back at Marge, as determined not to tell her everything as she was to try and discover it. "That's why she doesn't want to wait."

"Three weeks ago you told me your relationship was strictly platonic. You told everyone at the barbecue last Saturday the same thing."

Dillon shrugged again. "People have the right to change their minds."

Marge's jaw set. "It's not like you to be so hasty, Dillon."

For the first time in his life, Dillon resented Marge because she knew him so well. "Look, if it's going to cause a problem between us," he interjected, "I'll ask another couple to stand up for us on Saturday."

"No. Don't do that," Marge amended hastily.

"I don't want you hassling Hayley," he warned.

Marge met his dark look equably. "Afraid she might change her mind?" she taunted.

Dillon thought about the humiliation Hayley had suffered, because he'd made light of their living arrangements with the neighbors. "She won't change her mind," he said confidently. "And neither will I." They both knew they were doing what was right. They didn't need approval. Not even Marge's.

"YOU DON'T SEEM very nervous for someone who's about to be married," Marge observed.

*That's because it's not a real marriage,* Hayley thought as she smoothed her short, ivory silk dress over her hips. She gripped the nosegay of pale pink rosebuds and baby's breath in her hand and quipped lightly, "I guess I'm so calm because I've been this route before."

"Yes, but Dillon hasn't, and he's not nervous, either."

"I think I can remember when to say 'I do' without

having a nervous breakdown,'' Dillon said dryly, then pinched Marge's cheek with brotherly affection. He looked at her husband, Chuck. "Got the ring?"

Chuck patted his vest pocket. His face showed a moment's panic. Then he smiled with relief. "Yep." He thumped his silk-lined pocket emphatically. "It's right here, Dillon."

"There's more to marriage than just getting through the ceremony, Dillon," Marge retorted sternly.

Dillon winked audaciously, his sexy smile and the twinkle in his eyes leaving no doubt as to the libidinous nature of his thoughts. "I'm aware of that, too, Sis. And believe it or not, I think I'll know what Hayley wants me to do when the time comes."

Marge and Hayley both blushed at Dillon's bluntness.

Hayley gave him a dire look. They had agreed about this. No sex. She expected him to stick to his promise.

"I'm just worried the two of you are rushing into this," Marge told Hayley with familiar concern as they climbed the courthouse steps. Marge shifted Christine to her other hip. "But if you two are really so in love you can't wait another day, as Dillon said…"

Hayley had to fight to retain an inscrutable expression. Boy, he had really poured it on thick when he'd asked his sister and brother-in-law to witness their marriage.

"I mean," Marge continued, looking hard at both Dillon and Hayley, "if you're sure this is the right thing…"

Hayley looked at Dillon. He looked back at her. She thought of Christine's future and the money the sale of the house would bring her. She thought of the favor she'd be doing him in turning his house into a desirable home and the way this marriage was bound to stop the gossip in the neighborhood once and for all. She thought about living her dream, for one entire year, and knew it was what she wanted. "We're sure," she said softly, in unison with Dillon.

They smiled at each other, their minds made up.

Hayley and Dillon continued toward the judge's chambers.

"So in love…" Hayley murmured to Dillon under her breath. "Ha!"

Dillon gave her a sidelong glance. "Maybe you're right," he whispered back. "Maybe we should show them."

The next thing Hayley knew she'd been bent backward from the waist. Dillon threaded one hand through her hair. His lips grazed hers…tenderly at first, then with building passion. Hayley was inundated with so many sensations at once. The clean masculine scent of him, the minty taste of his mouth. And his lips, so sure and sensual, as they made a long, provocatively thorough tour of hers. Touching. Tasting. Teasing. My word, the man knew how to kiss. Knew how to exact a disturbing, thrilling, incredibly sensual response from her, the kind she had read about, dreamed about, but until now had never felt or even really expected to feel. And it was then, when Hayley realized what he'd done, that he slowly drew the disturbing caress to a halt.

Hayley stared up at him as he carefully guided her upright. Not sure she could stand unassisted, she clutched on to his arm, her fingers curving around his powerful biceps. Her heart slammed against her ribs, her breath came erratically and she stared up at him, flushing fiercely. "I can't believe you did that," she whispered, stunned.

"Neither can I! Dillon, you scoundrel you," Marge chided her brother. "Hiding the way you feel about her all this time! Well, after seeing the way the two of you kissed just now, I'm convinced!''

Unfortunately Hayley was convinced, too. Convinced she had made a terrible mistake. Convinced he was an incorrigibly sexy rogue, one she instinctively felt she would have a heck of a time handling. In a few short moments, Dillon had imbued her with more passion and excitement than she'd felt in a lifetime. How was she going to get through this? How was she going to stay married to him an entire year, live under the same roof with him and not...

Think about something else, she schooled herself firmly as she clutched her bouquet in damp fingers. But her stern lecture was of no use. His kiss was all she could think about during the entire wedding ceremony. She was so rattled, it was all she could manage to say "I do" in the proper places.

Not that she was supposed to really commit herself to Dillon under the circumstances. Still, it would have been nice, she thought, to believe for a little bit that their marriage could be a real one. Heaven knew a small, unrealistic part of her wanted a workable marriage.

Maybe it was because she was lonely and had been since Hank's death, she thought as Dillon slipped the ring on her finger, then she slipped the ring on his. And maybe, she thought nervously, it was something more.

"I pronounce you man and wife," the judge said happily.

*Oh, no,* Hayley thought.

"Dillon, you may kiss your bride."

To Hayley's utter astonishment, Dillon did it again. Oh, he didn't bend her backward from the waist this time, merely took her in his arms and fastened his mouth tenderly over hers, but the end result was all the same. She went perilously weak in the knees, and before she knew it she was kissing him back, just as sweetly. When he finally released her long seconds later, her emotions were completely awhirl. They remained that way as Marge handed her daughter back to her and the five of them exited the judge's chambers together.

He promised me we wouldn't make love, Hayley thought. He said this was to be a business arrangement only. But his kisses hadn't felt like any business arrangement. Oh, he'd meant business, all right, but not the kind they had agreed upon. Dillon meant the bedroom kind.

"Surprise!"

"What the—" Dillon said as they emerged from the courthouse. The whole neighborhood was on the steps, rice in hand.

"Marge told us about your eloping and we just had to come and wish you well." Carol beamed.

"We also know the two of you weren't even planning a weekend away," Hal continued.

"As I explained to Marge," Dillon said with a calm Hayley couldn't begin to feel, "we really just wanted to be alone together."

*Oh, no we don't,* Hayley thought. *I don't want to be alone with you for a second. Never mind anywhere near a bedroom.*

"And then there's Christine," Dillon continued affably. "And the new house—"

"Yes!" Hayley said. "We just have so much to do. Maybe later," she promised the group assembled on the steps, "we'll take a real honeymoon."

"But surely you and Dillon will accept our gift to you?" Nellie asked.

"Gift?" Dillon and Hayley echoed.

Dillon's sister Marge pointed to a gleaming white

stretch limousine at the curb. "Since you wouldn't let us give you a real reception, it's the least we could do. Everyone deserves a wedding supper to remember, with superb food, champagne and cake." She looked at her brother as if it were some kind of test. "And the two of you deserve to have it away from your home and all that renovating mess. You deserve to have a truly elegant meal."

"But Christine—" Hayley protested, feeling even more distressed.

"I'll take care of her," Marge said. She held out her arms and Christine went happily to Marge. "Chuck and I both will. In the meantime, you and Dillon both enjoy yourselves."

Dillon looked at Marge. Marge looked back at Dillon. They seemed to be having a silent battle of wills no one else was privy to. He doesn't like having his life arranged for him, Hayley thought. That was good because neither did she.

But to her horror, he merely sighed and said, "I guess you're right. Hayley and I do owe it to ourselves to take this time alone."

Ignoring the astonished look on Hayley's face and still holding tight to her hand, he zoomed down the steps. The next thing Hayley knew, she was being propelled into the waiting car, amidst a shower of rice and shouted good wishes.

Seconds later they pulled away from the curb and were off. Unable to believe he had not gotten them out of this, Hayley stormed, "I want to go home."

"You think I don't?" Dillon glanced at the pane of glass separating them from their driver. "But if we do that, the neighbors will know something's amiss. There will be even more talk." He sat back comfortably and stretched his long legs out in front of him. "And they'll be hugely offended because we didn't accept their very generous gift."

"Dillon—"

"One dinner, to celebrate our marriage," he announced pragmatically, his expression inscrutable. "What could it hurt?"

Plenty, Hayley thought, if the evening took even one mildly romantic turn. She'd already had two kisses from him in the space of thirty minutes. Was he planning a third?

Provoked he wasn't more upset with the turn of events, she accused, "You knew about this—"

"No. I'm as surprised as you. I, however, seem better able to take it in stride."

*You're not still quaking inside from unexpected kisses!* she thought. Unable to discuss that, however, Hayley said only, "You don't have a baby to worry about—"

"Don't try and con me, Hayley. Your nerves aren't about Christine. Marge has already watched Christine for you twice. Christine adores her. There's no one better with kids and you know it."

Her heart pounding, Hayley sat back in the limousine. This was all so unexpected. It didn't help that she was still reeling from the kisses.

She should have expected him to do something as crazy to convince everyone, his sister especially. But she hadn't. And even if she had, there was no way she could have been prepared for the warm evocative feel of his lips on hers, or the tingle of fire that had started in her lips, arrowed through her like lightning and gone straight to her toes. He kissed like he had a gift for it. And she didn't want to think about what else he might have a gift for.

"I was planning to finish retiling the kitchen this evening," Hayley asserted stubbornly.

Dillon glanced at her. Half his mouth slanted up in a knowing grin. "Sure that's all that's bothering you?" he taunted lightly. He narrowed his eyes and smiled. "Sure you're not afraid to be alone with me now that we're man and wife?"

"Don't be ridiculous!" Hayley fumed. "That ceremony didn't change anything. We're still exactly the same." Or were they? Her conscience prodded her mercilessly. Had his kisses and her unexpectedly ardent response changed everything? From the way she looked at him, to the way he looked at her. To the sensual turn this honeymoon dinner of theirs might take.

"If nothing's changed, what do you have to be so nervous about?" Dillon asked softly, his eyes holding hers.

She glared at him with scorn and suspicion.

"Besides," he sighed, "as long as we've been given the gift of an evening out, we might as well enjoy it." Dillon lifted a bottle of champagne from a bucket and popped the cork. "I intend to, anyway."

Her mouth unaccountably dry, Hayley watched him pour her a glass. Their fingers brushed as he handed it to her. She jumped and a little of the bubbly wine fizzed over the top and dribbled down her leg.

Dillon dabbed at her leg with the corner of a napkin, his action precise, methodical and, for Hayley, still unbearably exciting.

"Hayley, relax. I'm not going to jump your bones or anything." He winked and teased, "Not unless you want me to, that is."

Hayley took her glass and propelled herself as unobtrusively as possible into the seat opposite him. "Very funny."

He grinned like a cat who'd just lapped up a saucer of cream. "I thought so." He sat back in his seat. He let his gaze drift lazily over her as he sipped his champagne.

Hayley had thought it would be better, sitting away from him, instead of right next to him. But it was worse. Now she could see everything about him, from the rumpled layers of his chocolate brown hair to his straight nose and sensual mouth. The dark blue suit he wore made his eyes look navy, too. His jacket hung open, revealing the trim, taut lines of his middle beneath his shirt. She knew for a fact just how solid his chest was. She'd felt it pressed up against her during the brief, heady, but thoroughly convincing kiss that had followed their wedding ceremony. She knew why he'd kissed her like that, of course. To further fool Marge and Chuck. Still, it unnerved her. Maybe because she could still taste the unique flavor of his lips on hers. A compelling male flavor even several gulps of champagne couldn't wash away.

"Where are we going, anyway?" Hayley suddenly snapped at him. She hoped it wasn't too far. It would be dark soon.

"I'll ask."

He repeated her question to the driver through the intercom, then grinned.

"Well?" Hayley demanded, wishing she were as able to take this in stride as he was.

"He said it's a secret. We'll find out when we get there."

Hayley closed her eyes and groaned. "Not much for adventure, are you?" he bantered.

"Not this kind," she confessed, wondering why she'd ever thought marriage to Dillon could be simple. Clearly it was starting out to be anything but.

Dillon laughed again. He loosened his tie as the limousine headed onto the freeway. "Relax, Hayley. Knowing my sister and some of her friends, this evening is going to be very special indeed."

SPECIAL WASN'T THE word for it, Hayley thought several hours later as the limousine pulled up in front of a lakeside cottage at the end of a long graveled drive. "This doesn't look like any restaurant I've ever seen," Hayley muttered suspiciously.

Dillon frowned in consternation and swiftly retied his tie. "Wait here. I'll go check it out."

"Hold it. I have strict instructions you two lovebirds are to enter the building together," the chauffeur said.

Dillon was about to protest.

Not wanting to punish the driver, who was clearly just following the directions, Hayley put a hand to Dillon's arm before he could spout off. "Dillon, please," she said. "We've come this far." She took a deep, bracing breath. "We may as well go all the way. Besides, for all we know the whole neighborhood could be in there, waiting to jump out at us again and yell 'Surprise.'" At least she hoped that was the case.

Dillon stared at her. "You don't think—"

"What else could it be?" Hayley shrugged. "We didn't have a reception. You know how your sister carried on about that."

"There's no way you could fit a wedding party in that cottage."

"Then it can't be that bad." Hayley put on a stiff upper lip. "It's probably just a few people, or maybe some caterers to wait on us while we eat. Let's just go in and get it over with, okay?" Dillon didn't budge. "Okay?" she asked again, raising her brow in hopeful, prodding fashion.

"Ah, hell, as you said, we've come this far," Dillon muttered. Before she knew what was about to happen, he'd swung her up and into his arms. "Might as well go all the way."

"That's the spirit," the chauffeur said, applauding as Dillon strode up the walk toward the brightly burning lights.

Up the steps. Across the front porch of the gingerbread cottage. He paused at the door.

"It's open," the chauffeur called behind him.

"So it is," Dillon murmured. He pushed it open.

Inside, a fire was burning brightly in the hearth. A table for two was set with linen, silver, fine china and crystal. Another bouquet that matched the one she had carried served as the centerpiece. A note was propped up on one of the plates. It was addressed to "Dillon and Hayley."

Her heart sinking, Hayley watched Dillon open it. It seemed there was to be no crowded reception after all. "What does it say?" she asked.

"Hold your horses. I'm getting to that. 'Dear Dillon and Hayley,'" he read. "'Every newlywed couple deserves at least one night alone. The night, along with the superb wedding supper and all the privacy you could ever want, is yours. Enjoy. Love, Marge and the whole neighborhood.'"

"That does it." Hayley spun on her heel. "I am not spending a whole night out here alone."

"I agree." Dillon let the note flutter to the floor and beat her to the door. "This time my sister has gone too damn far with her meddling in my life. Who does she think she is?" He yanked open the door.

The limousine was gone.

Dillon stared at the empty gravel drive with astonishment. "Where the devil is that chauffeur?"

Hayley bent to pick up the note Dillon had dropped. Written on the back was a P.S. Her heart sinking, she read it to him. "'The chauffeur will be back to get you in the morning. Around ten.'"

"IT IS NOT MY FAULT there is no telephone here!" Dillon shouted.

"And I suppose it's not your fault there's only one bedroom, either," Hayley supposed. This was definitely more of an adventure than she'd bargained for.

"It was not my idea to get us stuck out here."

"And you think it was mine?" Hayley asked as she paced back and forth. She had agreed to marry him, not spend the night with him. They didn't even have her baby to distract them. If only they were home now. If only she could get back to working on her—she meant his—dream home. "I can't believe this is happening to me." All she had wanted was the chance to temporarily live a serene suburban life. Was that so terrible that she deserved this?

"Me, neither." Dillon stared around him morosely, looking just as suddenly miserable and sexually on edge as she felt. He turned to her grimly. "The Jets are playing tonight."

Hayley rolled her eyes, incensed he could actually be thinking about sports at a time like this! "Oh, please. Am I supposed to feel sorry for you?"

Dillon shrugged. "Think what you like, but the evening would be a heck of a lot more bearable if we had a TV."

Hayley couldn't disagree with that. As it was, they had virtually nothing to distract them from each other. Nothing to keep them from thinking about those two very sensual kisses he had given her, or the passionate way she had responded. They didn't even have a telephone book to read.

But they did have their common sense. And both were far too wise to let anything potentially uncomfortable happen between them now that they were both on the brink of having everything they wanted. Hayley, her dream of living in the suburbs with her baby. Dillon, a housekeeper to whip his place into shape, and a house he would eventually be able to sell for an enormous profit.

Aware the air was scented with mouth-watering aromas and that she hadn't eaten for hours, Hayley glanced at the sideboard. "I wonder what we're having for dinner," she murmured. Eating would at least keep them busy for a little while.

Dillon perked up at the thought of a diversion. "There's one way to find out." He strode to the refrigerator and flung it open.

Looking over his shoulder, Hayley saw it had been well stocked with every delicacy imaginable. The wine rack on the counter was full of a collection of domestic and imported wine and champagne.

Dillon pulled out a salad. Jerking loose the knot of his tie with one hand, he carried it to the table. "Let's get this over with," he growled.

"Get what over with?" Hayley asked, her mouth dry and her heart pounding.

"What do you think? Dinner!" he replied.

Acting as trapped and unhappy as Hayley felt, Dillon yanked the tie from around his neck. He crumpled it up in one hand and tossed it onto the sofa. "I'm going to go ahead and eat now." He unplugged a silver chafing dish of simmering boeuf bourguignonne and brought it to the table. "And I'd suggest you do the same." His lips compressed grimly. He met her eyes frankly. "Unless I miss my guess or you change your attitude, this is going to be one long night."

"You're blaming me for this mess?" Hayley asked, astonished.

"I think you could be a little more cooperative, yes."

"Cooperative, how?" she ground out.

"Pleasant."

"I am being pleasant," Hayley defended herself hotly. "As pleasant as I know how."

The mischievous glimmer in his eyes said she wasn't. "But not nearly as pleasant and acquiescent as you were when I kissed you at the courthouse."

Hayley folded her arms at her waist. "I don't want to talk about that!" she stormed.

"Yeah," Dillon uttered a lazy sigh, "I didn't figure you would."

"What does that mean?"

Dillon shrugged his broad shoulders. "Just that you don't seem to want to deal with things as they are."

"And how are they?"

He leaned toward her earnestly, his entire attention focused on her. "You responded to my kisses, Hayley." He gave her a very knowing, very male grin. "Hell, by the second time, you were even kissing me back."

"I was caught off guard—"

"Yeah." He grinned, all scoundrel again. "And you liked it, too, didn't you?"

Her cheeks burning with the heat of her embarrassment, Hayley kept her eyes firmly on his and pushed the words through her teeth. "I am not going to discuss this with you."

He leveled a very direct, very probing gaze back at her. "Why not?" he taunted in a velvety soft voice.

"Because—" Hayley drew a deep breath, more determined than ever to win back control of the situation and her heart. "It's not going to happen again, Dillon." She would not be loved and left by a roving newsman, anxious to be back on the international beat.

"You're sure about that?" Dillon pinned her down in the same soft, self-confident voice.

She met his eyes, and although she was quaking inside, somehow managed to overcome her fear and her desire and give a short, stiff nod. "Very sure," she said.

For a second, a flicker of hurt was reflected in his dark blue eyes. It was gone as quickly as it had appeared, making Hayley wonder if she'd really seen it there at all. Or had she just wanted to see it?

"Fine, have it your way," Dillon said. He sat down at the table and spread his napkin across his lap.

Feeling even more panicked at the prospect of the whole night looming before them, she demanded, "Well? Aren't you going to do something to get us out of here?" He was a newsman with years of experience. He was resourceful. He ought to have picked up some tricks along the way.

"Like what?" His mood curiously remote, almost offended, he reached for her plate and ladled tender strips of beef onto it.

Hayley slid reluctantly into the chair opposite him, unwilling to admit how hungry she was, or how romantic a setting the small, cozy lakeside cottage was. If this hadn't been a cruel twist of fate, if her marriage had been a real one instead of a convenient business arrangement, she would have enjoyed being stranded here with him and considered it idyllically romantic. But it wasn't a real marriage, and this wasn't a real honeymoon, she reminded herself sternly.

"We could hike to the nearest phone," she finally said. Dillon frowned and broke open a soft, fragrant roll.

"It's at least ten miles to the nearest gas station. There's no guarantee it'd be open when we got there."

"So? We could at least try, Dillon."

"Hayley, it's one night." He regarded her with a mixture of exasperation and aggravation. "We'll live."

Would they? They had no clothes, nothing to distract them from each other or from what this night was supposed to be. There was one bed visible in the bedroom beyond. It was a double. One bath. He was still thinking about their kisses and her response. He'd made no secret of the fact he would like their relationship to go even further.

Her mouth dry as dust, Hayley picked up her fork. While she picked desultorily at the beef on her plate, Dillon dug into his with gusto. He glanced up at her. Without warning, his face gentled sympathetically. "How about some wine?"

Hayley hesitated. Wine would relax her. It would also lessen her inhibitions, thereby making her more susceptible to any advances he might choose to make.

"Suit yourself," he said brusquely when she hesitated, looking offended again. "But I'm having some."

"Thank you, I'll pass," Hayley said. Whatever happened tonight, she wasn't going to blame it on the wine. She had the feeling she needed all her senses working at optimum efficiency tonight, if she were to keep him at arm's length.

He finished his meal in record time and leaned back in his chair. He tipped his head to one side and regarded her. "Are you always such a stick-in-the-mud?" Dillon asked.

"I beg your pardon?"

"Haven't you ever been stranded anywhere before?"

"As a matter of fact, I have," Hayley said stiffly. She

didn't know why she'd ever thought he was a gentleman. Clearly he was anything but civilized.

"When?" he asked with a grin.

"When I was a child."

"Yeah?" Challenge lit his eyes. He seemed to be daring her not to bore him. "What happened?"

Memories assaulted Hayley. None of them good. "Okay, once I was at the skating rink. My parents were supposed to come pick me and a friend up at four o'clock. They didn't show." Her glance collided with Dillon's. Unable to bear the mixture of curiosity and sympathy in his dark blue gaze, she was the first to look away. "We tried calling my home, but there was no answer, so we called my friend's folks. And they came to pick us up. It was only later—" the color left her face "—that I found out about the car accident that had claimed their lives."

She pushed her chair away from the table; her chair scraped noisily across the floor. Her face pale, she rushed to the window, where she stood staring out at the darkness of the night and the moonlight shimmering off the surface of the lake.

Dimly aware he'd never felt more stupid or helpless in his life, Dillon bolted after her. Then once he was at her side, he hung back. The stiff set of her shoulders let him know she didn't want to be touched. And after the way he'd been treating her, he knew he could hardly blame her.

He hadn't meant to kiss her. He didn't even know why he had. Except that his attraction to her, and hers to him, had been building. She had looked so pretty in her short, ivory silk wedding dress and still did. It was a romantic kind of day, his wedding day, and probably the only wedding he would ever have. And even if it hadn't been a real one in the strictest sense of the word, he'd still wanted the day to be special. He'd wanted to prove to Marge and Chuck they had no reason to worry, he knew exactly what he was doing. Only now he wasn't sure about that. He hadn't figured on quite so much passion. Hadn't figured on her melting against him, when he'd kissed her, like butter on a hot stove, the moment he took her in his arms. Hadn't figured he would still ache to hold her in his arms again.

Damn it all, he wanted to kiss her. Not just once, but again and again and again. And yet he knew if he did, chances were this time it wouldn't end quite so simply. "Hayley, I'm sorry."

"Thanks."

"Not just about your folks." He paused. "I've been giving you a hard time tonight because I'm so aggravated with Marge for getting us into this mess—"

"I know how you feel about that," Hayley interjected, with a single heartfelt glance.

"And I'm aggravated with myself, too." Dillon continued his confession flatly. He watched her eyes widen in surprise, then finished more gently, "I know if I'd told Marge the whole truth about us in the first place we wouldn't be here now. She would have found a tactful way to stop the neighbors."

"Maybe, maybe not," Hayley said with a deadpan look. "I have a feeling Marge wants us together. I think she's been matchmaking from the start. Not that it'll do her any good," Hayley amended hastily. "And as for my parents and what happened to them." She tilted her head away from his. "It's okay, Dillon. I've had a long time to come to terms with that and—and I have."

She didn't look like she'd come to terms with anything, Dillon thought. Never mind those years she had spent growing into adulthood without her folks. Still aching to hold her, he had no choice but to respect her need for space. He moved back slightly, and for want of anything better to do with them, shoved his hands deep into the pockets of his trousers. "How old were you when you lost your parents?" he asked.

"Nine." Hayley paced away from him across the room.

"What happened to you after that?"

Hayley shrugged. "I lived with a lot of different relatives. My father came from a large family. Unlike him and my mother, his brothers and sisters all had lots of children."

Dillon knew there was much she wasn't saying. "Did your relatives take good care of you?"

"They tried, but my whole family lived in the city, in apartments. There wasn't much room. Even though they loved me, I never stayed anywhere for very long, and I always tried to be as helpful as I could be while I was there."

No wonder Hayley was so fiercely independent, so determined to make a separate, stable life for herself and her daughter. In her place he would've been, too. "Which is how you came to know construction," Dillon surmised.

"And a dozen other useful and not-so-useful things." Hayley smiled. "How did we get onto this subject, anyway?" she asked huskily.

"How else? My insensitivity."

"We really don't know very much about each other, do we, Dillon?"

Dillon had thought he'd known everything that was important about her. That she was pretty, practical and hot-tempered. Not to mention endlessly resourceful and independent to a fault. Tonight, for the first time, he saw there was more, much more, beneath her surface unflappability. "That could change," Dillon said hopefully.

Hayley stepped back, her expression neutral. "You know what? I think—" She hesitated, her eyes lifting briefly to his, then swiftly evading, ending the intimacy they'd shared as abruptly as it had begun. "I think I'd like to go to bed, if you don't mind," she finished.

Dillon knew she was running. He couldn't help but feel disappointed, rejected, even. But he also knew he had no right to insist she stay up with him. Generally, the less he knew about the women he took to bed, or even thought about taking to bed, the better. It made it easier to break off with them when the time came. And because of the nature of his job, the time always came to move on. Still, he wanted to know Hayley.

He suddenly frowned. "Though what we're going to do about clothes—" He left the thought hanging and sighed, as he considered sleeping in his suit. Or worse, sleeping without the suit. Ten to one, after the way he'd kissed her earlier today, Hayley wouldn't appreciate him running around in his underwear.

"They left us food. Maybe they left us robes in the bedroom."

Knowing his sister's highly romantic streak, Dillon shuddered to think what might have been left. Seconds later, as Hayley came out of the bedroom, he found out. Looped over one arm was a silk bathrobe and matching pajama pants. "I think these belong to you."

The clothing sailed through the air. He caught the garments with one hand. "That satisfies half my curiosity." He wiggled his eyebrows; deep down, he really wanted to see Hayley's outfit. "What are you wearing?"

"Never you mind about that, Dillon Gallagher," she chided.

"Sexy, huh?" He grinned.

Hayley's blush confirmed his guess that his sister had probably shopped for Hayley at Victoria's Secret.

"You'll never know," she taunted. With a saucy toss of her head, she sashayed purposefully back into the bedroom. The door shut behind her with a soft thud.

Dillon grinned and put his feet up. He wasn't sure why—in light of the fact he'd just been rejected romantically—but he was feeling cheerful again. Content. Almost upbeat. Relieved, too.

Maybe because Hayley was right not to take any chances he'd end up in her bed tonight. After all, there was no sense in rushing things unnecessarily. They had a whole year together. A year in which they would be *man and wife*. The chance for them to be together would come soon enough. And when it did...

Dillon pictured it and grinned again.

# Chapter Five

Hayley had to hand it to Marge, as she sank ever deeper into the steamy bubble bath, scented liberally with White Linen perfume. Her sister-in-law had thought of everything. White wicker baskets of His and Hers toiletries had been left in the bath. The old-fashioned feather bed looked soft and inviting, just big enough for two. And the lingerie she'd left for Hayley! Hayley blushed just thinking about the gossamer sheerness of the long, white gown, with its brief, lacy bodice and bare back.

She had everything she needed for a perfect wedding night *except* a man to make wild, passionate love to her. She shut her eyes and tried not to think about how much Dillon's kisses had affected her. She had only to remember and she trembled.

Not that it was really any surprise to her she'd reacted that way. She'd been incredibly attracted to Dillon from the first, more attracted than she had been to any man. Including Hank. And that scared her. If Dillon decided to put the moves on her, she wasn't sure she could say no.

She sighed, her heart aching as she thought about how long it had been since anyone had held her close or whispered sweet nothings into her ear, how long it had been since she'd felt really beautiful, really loved. She made jokes about it, of course, declaring to anyone who would listen to her that she was not a lonely widow, but the truth was, she *was* lonely.

She had no doubt, of course, that Dillon could be persuaded to fill the sensual void in her life with precious little encouragement. She'd seen the way he looked at her, felt the chemistry between them on more than one occasion and sensed that he would be a superb, inventive lover.

But she'd already been married once to a man whose devotion to his career had taken precedence over her. No, she was older and wiser now. She knew she wanted a cozy home in the suburbs, a safe place to rear her daughter, and a job she loved. And if some small hedonistic part of her was tempted to give in to the desire she felt for Dillon, especially on a night like tonight, then so be it. It didn't mean she had to *do* anything about it.

Hayley stepped out of the bath and blotted herself dry with a thick fluffy towel. She had managed without any sort of man-woman intimacy in her life for the last year. For the sake of her dream, she could continue to do so during the next.

All that mattered was the deal she'd made with Dillon and the financial freedom the successful sale of his house would bring her, she decided as she smoothed on White Linen lotion in generous strokes. She would concentrate on the house and her plans for it. She let her hair down and brushed it into a soft golden cloud about her shoulders. She wouldn't think about Dillon, or her growing desire. She wouldn't think about his kisses, or the sensual fulfillment he could give her.

DILLON HAD NEVER PLANNED to have a wedding night, ever, but if he'd had one, this certainly wasn't how he would have envisioned himself spending it: tossing and turning on an uncomfortably hard couch a foot and a half too short for him.

It didn't help that he could hear Hayley tossing and turning in the squeaky bed in the next room, or smell the soft, womanly drift of her perfume. She was off-limits to him. They'd both agreed about that. And he was a man who kept his word.

Trouble was, he was damn near tempted to break that word, to simply go into the next room, take her in his arms and find out if there was as much sizzle between them as he suspected.

When he'd first met her, he'd noticed how attractive she was. Hell, even a monk would have done that. He folded his arms behind his head and grinned, thinking about how she'd warned him, right off, not to do a merry widow routine on her. Yet something in the feisty set of her chin had told him she'd been through the ringer since Hank's death.

And like it or not, he did feel responsible about that. He scowled, irritated with himself. Because he'd been Hank's mentor and friend, Dillon was stepping in for him, that's all. He was taking pains to see that Hank's widow and baby were set for the future. Having Hayley work for him was an added bonus....

But that arrangement hadn't turned out the way he'd envisioned. He'd expected her to be more wifely somehow, more intent on fixing him breakfast and dinner no matter how he protested. Instead, all she seemed to really care about, besides Christine of course, was the damned house. Every waking minute of her days and nights were spent ripping out floor tile, carpet and old wallpaper.

Maybe if he hadn't been such a jerk at the block barbecue, they'd be a lot closer now. Maybe if he hadn't let the other guys assume he and Hayley were already lovers, she would be amenable to the idea of them as lovers now. But he had, and she wasn't. So here he was. Married. Stuck on the damned sofa. On his honeymoon.

His sister would sure laugh if she ever found out what was going on right now. She'd tell him he was only getting what he deserved after so many years of drifting from one woman to the next. Not that he felt he'd mistreated anyone. He'd always parted on good terms. Perhaps because he had been so honest about wanting only a physical relationship.

He sensed it wasn't going to be that easy with Hayley though. He was already getting closer to her than he felt comfortable doing. And yet it was hard not to do otherwise whenever he was around her, whenever he found himself looking into her jade green eyes.

He could still hear her moving in the next room. He shut his eyes. How in the world was he going to sleep under these circumstances?

HAYLEY WOKE shortly after two, shivering with cold and wondering what Dillon was doing. Too late, she realized several things. The cottage did not have central heat, or if it did, the thermostat wasn't set very high. She should have eaten her dinner because she was ravenously hungry now.

If only Dillon weren't here, she would get up, go into the other room, raid the refrigerator, stoke up the fire and then go back to bed. If only she had a robe, she might venture out there, anyway. But she didn't.

All she had on was the very sexy nightgown. She did, however, have one of the comforters that had originally been on the bed. She could very easily wrap up in that. Dillon would never see her gown.

Satisfied she had a suitably modest way to proceed, she went to the door and stood against it, listening. She heard nothing. No sounds of any kind. Nor was there any light coming from beneath the door.

Quietly she slid open the door. Dillon was sound asleep, his large form sprawled on the sofa, the comforter tangled down around his knees. One arm was flung above his head, the other was folded across his waist. Both legs were bent in slightly, to fit on the sofa. The knee closest to the back of the sofa was upraised. The sound of his deep, steady breathing filled the room.

She moved as quietly and stealthily as possible around the sofa. She looked at him, to make sure he was really as deeply asleep as he appeared, before she began her task. And once she had started looking she couldn't seem to stop.

He was so handsome, even in his sleep! The relaxed set of his features in no way detracted from the ruggedness of his face. He was a man's man, in action, thought, deed and, yes, she thought smiling down at the agreeably rumpled layers of his dark hair, even in sleep. His skin was golden beneath the shadow of his evening beard. His dark thick lashes looked silkier and longer than ever. She felt a moment's disappointment, not being able to gaze into his navy blue eyes. But that faded as her gaze drifted lower to his sensual mouth.

Her insides tingled as she recalled his kisses. He'd been fully clothed then, but she had still felt the hardness of his chest. Now he was shirtless and she saw the bunched muscles. They were covered with whorls of curling dark brown hair that arrowed down into the waistband of his silk pajama pants. The dark silk rode low, beneath his navel, and stretched across his abundant sex, detailing everything.

For a second, she imagined how it would feel to be held against him now, with only the thin barriers of chiffon and silk between them, then she pushed the disturbing fantasy away. Thoughts like this would not help her get back to sleep. Instead, they would keep her up all night.

She needed to get back to business. She moved past him and knelt before the dwindling embers of the fire. One hand still clutching the comforter she had wrapped about her shoulders, she reached for the fire screen, then drew back. There was no way she could remove the metal screen, stoke up the fire, add another log and replace the screen, all without being heard, not if she just used one hand. She would need both her hands. That meant dropping the quilt.

She cast another look behind her to make sure Dillon was still asleep. He was. Shivering with the cold, she shrugged off the comforter and turned her attention back to the fireplace. With two hands she silently removed the screen and set it aside. Reaching for a log, she positioned it crosswise over the dying fire. She reached for the poker and stirred up the flames. Satisfied, Hayley replaced the poker in the rack, sat a moment soaking in the warmth and then put back the screen.

"Nice job," Dillon said softly.

Still on her knees, she pivoted and looked directly into his dark blue eyes. She gasped and her hand flew to her throat. "I didn't know you were awake."

"That makes us even." Dillon untangled his legs and flung back the covers. He flashed her an easy smile. "I didn't know you were cold." He grimaced and moved stiffly as he rose.

Hayley felt a lightning bolt of guilt. "The sofa's that uncomfortable?"

"Well." He shrugged his bare shoulders and flashed

her another sexy smile. "Not as comfortable as the bed, I'm sure, but just as cold." He shivered as the cool air assaulted his bare chest and he hunkered down beside her. She saw his nipples contract in the mat of thick, dark chest hair. Her lower abdomen felt oddly heavy. It pulsed wildly with the rhythm of her heartbeat.

"Damn Marge for not renting a place with central heating," he managed.

Despite the chill of the cottage, Hayley felt a trickle of perspiration between her breasts and prayed Dillon wouldn't notice. Turning away from him, she crossed her arms in front of her and rubbed her hands on her arms to generate some warmth.

"'Course," Dillon continued, "they probably figured with the two of us in one bed, the bedroom door opened, the fire burning, that we'd be plenty warm enough."

"True," Hayley said. The room was dark, except for the glow of the fire. But in the moonlight, he could see she was wearing an incredibly sexy, lacy white nightgown that looked as wispy as chiffon and was just as sheer. The spaghetti straps bared the lustrous skin of her slender shoulders as well as the enticing upper curves of her breasts and the deep shadowy valley between them.

Dillon swallowed. The heart-shaped bodice hugged the fullness of her breasts, clearly delineating the soft, rounded globes and dusky rose centers. From there, the gown hugged her ribs, nipped in at the waist and flared out at the hips. A slit in one side of the gown, from ankle to mid-hip, bared one very long, very sexy leg. Dillon didn't have to look at the shadowy golden vee between her legs to know she was naked beneath. The blood rushed to his groin. It was all he could do not to groan aloud.

"Nice outfit," he drawled lazily, to cover the fast-growing ache inside him. "You ought to wear it more often."

Hayley swiftly drew the comforter around her shoulders and aimed a killer look at him. "Very funny."

"I thought so." He liked the droll humor in her voice and the exasperated warmth he saw flowing into her cheeks. And he especially liked the way her honey blond hair was spilling over her shoulders and glowing silver in the soft moonlight.

"Hungry?" he asked. Not waiting for her to answer, he said, "I am." He strode barefoot to the refrigerator and brought out two wicker gift baskets filled with gourmet treats. He handed them to her then went back for a bottle of diet soda and two long-stemmed champagne glasses.

"You know, if you'd eaten your dinner like a good girl this wouldn't happen to you," he teased. He set more goodies on the coffee table and moved it and the sofa closer to the fire.

Hayley sank down nervously onto one corner of the sofa. It was still warm with his body heat. It felt oddly sensual to her, sitting where he had recently slept. "What wouldn't have happened to me? Getting stranded with you in the middle of nowhere or waking up in the middle of the night?"

"I *am* your new husband," he reminded, as he unwrapped a petit four, handed it to her, then poured soda in the long-stemmed glasses.

"Why this and not the champagne?" Hayley asked.

He shrugged. Rummaging around behind him on the sofa, he finally located his robe and drew it on. Not bothering to tie it, or even draw the edges closed, he picked up his glass. "I don't want you to think I'm trying to make you lose your senses.'' It was going to be hard enough not to seduce her as it was.

Hayley tried to look away from the wide strip of hard male flesh exposed from neck to navel. She tried hard not to notice his firm silky skin or the way the silk clung to the most masculine part of his anatomy. She raised her glance to his and held it there. ''Is that usually how you operate?'' she asked lightly.

''Well, I do usually try to get women—uh—relaxed.'' He grinned wickedly.

''I'm serious,'' Hayley protested, knowing Dillon well enough by now to realize he would never willfully take advantage of any woman. He wouldn't have to. He would, however, go after what he wanted with no holds barred.

''Seriously? I like women conscious.''

''I'll bet.''

Dillon merely grinned. He stretched out beside her, lifted an edge of her comforter and slid in beside her, so they were situated shoulder-to-shoulder in the warmth. With his free hand, he pulled the other comforter out from beneath him and spread it over their legs, so the two of them were fully cocooned. Yet the pass Hayley half expected and knew she wanted, at least in a strictly hedonistic sense, never came.

They ate awhile in silence, consuming grapes, crackers, cheese and more of the delicious petits fours. Finally, when both couldn't eat a bit more, they pushed the picnic basket away. Dillon replenished their glasses with chilled diet soda. They put their feet up on the coffee table.

''Dillon?''

''Hmm?'' He sounded as drowsy and content as she felt.

''Do you think we made a mistake? Getting married today?''

Dillon turned to her, his shoulder nudging hers beneath the blanket. "Does it feel like a mistake?"

"It doesn't feel like being married," she confessed.

Dillon looked as if he'd had an enormous weight removed from his shoulders. He heaved a relieved sigh. "Good."

Hayley stared into the flickering flames of the fire and tried not to take offense at the sheer depth of his relief. "I know what you mean. I don't want to be trapped in anything, either."

"But?"

"I guess I just wish…" Her voice dwindled off. She wished he weren't under the blanket with her. She wished they both weren't so warm or cozy.

"What?" Dillon slid a hand beneath her chin and tilted her face up to his.

"I don't know." Hayley resisted the urge to draw back. She swallowed around the sudden dryness of her throat. "Well, it's complicated, Dillon." She turned her head and looked away.

He dropped his hand back to his lap. "Tell me, anyway," he persuaded her.

Hayley continued to stare at the fire. The flames were as blue as Dillon's eyes. She wet her lips. "My life wasn't supposed to turn out this way."

He shrugged, his shoulder nudging hers. "I think mine just took an unexpected left turn, too."

"It doesn't bother you?"

He stretched his legs out even farther in front of him. "I live for the moment. I always have." He slouched down, so the back of his head rested against the top of the sofa. "I thought you did, too."

"Did," she corrected. "Can't anymore."

"Because of Christine?"

"Yes."

Dillon's glance narrowed. He studied her bluntly. "Maybe that's not so wise," he said after a moment.

His criticism was casual, impersonal. Yet it stung more than she would've expected it to. "What do you mean?" Hayley asked, aware her heart was pounding in her throat again and that he was very, very close to her. Close enough for her to inhale the intoxicatingly male scent of his skin and cologne.

"Maybe you shouldn't do literally everything for her," Dillon said, capturing her hand with his own. He held it tightly. "Maybe you should do some things for yourself, too."

"Like what?"

"Like this."

His mouth covered hers and she lost her breath at the first touch. Everything around her went soft and fuzzy except the hard, hot pressure of his mouth.

With a low moan of satisfaction, Dillon threaded his hand through the hair at the nape of her neck and angled her head so their kiss could deepen. His other hand pressed against her spine, urging her closer, until her breasts were against his chest. He ran his hand up and down her spine.

He was generating flames of heat, tremors of arousal, and with them, Hayley realized, came the need to be so much closer. The slow, hot, gentle strokes of his tongue were unbearably sweet, unbearably seductive, unbearably intimate. Unable to help herself, she began to return his kisses, shyly at first, then with growing ardor. This was heaven, she thought. Certainly, the nearest she'd ever come.

And yet there were so many reasons, her baby the least among them, why she shouldn't let this continue, Hayley thought. "Dillon," Hayley moaned. "You promised. We said we wouldn't...oh..." She shuddered as he touched her breast, cupped it warmly with his hand and worked the nipple to an aching crown. Fire shot through her, as elemental as the night.

"I know." He gathered her in a persuasive embrace. "But that was before I saw you in that nightgown," he whispered as his mouth moved expertly over hers, evoking another freefall of sensation. His hands caressed her shoulders, moved tenderly over the bare skin of her back. "God, you're beautiful in the firelight, Hayley."

Hayley couldn't help it. She closed her eyes. *So are you. So is this.*

Her mouth was pliant beneath his, warm and sexy. Dillon put everything he had into the kiss, knowing this was his one chance to show Hayley how their lovemaking could be. Chemistry like theirs came along once in a lifetime—*maybe.* He was determined to savor this while it lasted.

"You don't even know me, Dillon," she protested. The pleasure he was bringing her was so sweet, so unexpected, so total, it was all she could do to keep from moaning again.

"I know enough to know I want you," he murmured hotly. Once again his hands moved to her breasts. "Now all we have to find out is if you want me, too."

He kissed her as he had during the wedding ceremony—firmly, with a deft, sure touch. His mouth was hot, the abrasion of his evening beard like fine-grained sandpaper against her face.

"Oh, sweetheart," he murmured, his arms tightening around her until her breasts were crushed again against the hardness of his chest.

The scent of his cologne, so brisk and piney and evocatively male, filled her senses. Hayley opened her mouth. His tongue slipped inside, delving deep. Another arrow of fire shot through her. She tried to fight it and failed, then moaned as the strength left her body. She trembled with desire.

"Dillon," she murmured, trying to struggle free.

"Don't fight me, Hayley," he whispered, raining kisses down her neck, across her collarbone and the uppermost swell of her breasts. He pushed aside the gossamer fabric, baring one shoulder. His lips traced a fiery, erotic path. "Don't fight the pleasure."

And then his mouth was on hers again, plundering with a voracious intensity Hayley simply could not fight. She kissed him back; she gave up the struggle. Dillon was right. She did want this, had for hours.

Dillon swept her up into his arms. He carried her into the bedroom and laid her gently on the bed. "If we're going to do this, we're going to be comfortable," he vowed huskily, stripping off his pajama bottoms and his robe.

Hayley stared, entranced, as he lay down next to her. He was beautiful, all sleek, supple, naked male. His arousal, so hot and hard, pressed against her thigh.

"Let me see you." Dillon guided the gown off her shoulder. He bared a breast, laved it with his tongue, blew it dry with his breath. Hayley arched against him restlessly, needing more.

"I know, sweetheart," Dillon whispered. Eager to please her, he swiftly bared her other breast. His thumbs and fingers playing over her nipples until they were tight, aching peaks and her knees fell open.

He pushed her gown above her waist and slid a hand between her thighs. She cried out as he touched her. She arched her back as heat spread through her in mesmerizing, undulating waves. "Oh, Dillon," she whispered, drawing his mouth back down to hers. "Dillon..." She couldn't believe how he was making her feel. She never wanted it to stop. Never.

Nor apparently did he, Hayley thought, as he made a rough impatient sound low in his throat and smothered her cries with his kisses. And all the while his hand stroked, explored, until she was silky wet, exploding with rhythmic, volcanic force. He angled his body up against her softness.

"Damn, Hayley," he whispered breathlessly against her mouth, "you're wild. And wonderful. Just like I knew you would be." Sure now she was ready, he slid inside her.

Hayley arched against him, her hips undulating beneath his. She held him close. Her palms cupped his shoulders.

He answered her by going even deeper. So deep Hayley cried out, as did he. She ran her hands up and down his back, digging her fingers into the hard straining muscles, and clamped her legs around his waist, pulling him toward her. He murmured her name and buried his fingers in her hair. His arm curved around her hips and lifted her even higher, so her lower body was pressed tightly, irrevocably against his.

Her universe shattered. And then, as her common sense slowly and inevitably returned, she grew very, very still.

"IT WAS A MISTAKE." Hayley declared, her gossamer gown a damp, love-stained tangle around her middle.

"Mistake?" Dillon echoed, his eyes trailing over her mussed hair and lower still, past her face, past her chin. Lower still.

She followed the direction of his gaze and glanced down self-consciously. Her breasts were bared. The nipples were rosy and erect. She couldn't have advertised the pleasure she'd experienced at his hands more if she'd taken out an ad in the *Times!*

Her humiliation now as complete as his lovemaking had been, Hayley flushed from head to toe. Dillon grinned, looked even more content. Hastily she righted her gown, pushing it back on her shoulders, over her breasts and down past her waist.

"Yes, Dillon, it was a mistake. An *accident,*" Hayley clarified, as she willfully put their conversation back on track. She sent him a furious look. "It'll never happen again."

"Well, that's a new one," he drawled, reclining on the bed. He was gloriously naked and as unashamed of his body as she was inherently modest. "If that's what it feels like to have an 'accident' with you, I volunteer to have a head-on collision anytime."

Infuriated, Hayley jumped up. She stood beside the bed. To her dismay, the preemptive action only served to make her more acutely aware of the ongoing tingling in her lower body. She clamped down hard on her senses, telling herself she was not still aroused! Fortunately Dillon's smug expression gave her the strength she so desperately needed. She studied him resolutely. "Honestly, Dillon. You didn't think that—just because we—this isn't a real marriage."

"No," he smiled naughtily, "but one with some definite perks."

"Get out!"

"I don't think so." He lounged against the pillows, feeling more content and relaxed than he had in years. "Not until we talk this out."

"Please put on your clothes. There's nothing to talk out."

"Maybe you're right." He folded his hands behind his head and propped one knee up. "Actions always do speak louder than words."

"Then read this!" She tossed his pajama pants in his face.

Grinning, he palmed them, but made no effort to slip them on. "You sure are upset."

"You noticed."

"Oh, I noticed all right. It'd be hard not to with you pacing back and forth like a caged lioness. What I don't understand is what the big deal is—" He straightened and swung his legs over the side of the bed.

Hayley tore her eyes from his generously endowed form. She raked her hands through her hair. "The big deal, you idiot, is we just consummated our marriage."

"Now hold on." He held up a palm, traffic cop fashion. Finally his face paled to the parchment hue of hers. "We're in a gray area there."

Knowing he was now as terrified by the future legal ramifications of what they'd done as she, was little comfort to Hayley. "Oh, I don't know." She mocked his earlier drawl to a tee. "What we just did seemed pretty plain to me. It's called—"

"*Terrific* is the word I think you're looking for," he interrupted.

Yes, it had been, but she would never let him know that. "Under any definition of the law—" she began tightly.

"Lovemaking is a normal part of any marriage contract."

"Not ours, and it wasn't lovemaking."

"It sure felt like lovemaking to me." He knew it hadn't been simple sex. Simple sex left you empty. Sexually drained, but empty. What he and Hayley had shared had left him wanting more. A far sight more.

"Damn it, Dillon." She flung her arms out to her sides. "This ruins everything."

Her rising hysteria made it easier for him to remain calm. "I don't see how," he said practically, drawing on his pajama pants. "We still have our prenuptial agreement. You'll still get your money from the house."

"And in the meantime?"

He shrugged and pulled on his robe, again leaving it open. He stood and sent her a sexy grin. "In the meantime, we just found a way to make living together under the same roof more bearable. In fact, it might even be fun!"

Hayley stepped back so fast she crashed into the bureau. "No!"

"Why not?" Dillon put out a hand to steady her.

"Because," Hayley stormed, shaking off his gentle touch and looking even more upset.

He let his hand drop slowly to his side. "Because why?"

She sent him a withering glare. "Because things are starting to get too complicated," she said with mounting impatience.

He could see she was irked because he didn't agree with her; he didn't care. "They don't have to be," he retorted easily. "I want you. You want me."

"Did want you," Hayley corrected, looking down her nose at him. She harrumphed haughtily. "I don't now."

That was a lie, Dillon thought victoriously. And one day soon he would prove it to them both. But not now. If he did so now, she would turn and run. "If you say so." His eyes gleamed.

"And stop looking at me like that," she snapped, running her fingers through the tousled waves of her honey blond hair.

"Like what?" He watched as Hayley clamped her arms beneath her breasts. The action lifted them, made them swell above the lacy edge of her bodice. Dillon grimaced as he felt the blood rush to his groin once again.

"Like you're going to seduce me again."

Dillon moved away from her before his baser instincts got the better of him. "Hey! I didn't seduce you."

"You put the moves on me."

"And you put them on me right back!"

She moaned. "Talking about it is just making it worse."

He looked down at his fly, and lower, to the hard ridge of flesh. He sighed audibly and couldn't help but remark, "Gotta agree with you there."

Hayley turned bright red. She dropped her hands. "Forget it," she warned grimly, giving him a killer look. "I have a headache that's going to last for the next whole year."

Dillon laughed, and though he was very tempted to prove her a liar here and now, thought better of it and sauntered out lazily. "We'll see," he promised.

Hayley marched after him, her bare feet smacking against the floor. She leaned in the door, her hands gripping the wood on either side of her, but didn't go any farther into the next room.

"What do you mean, we'll see?" Hayley demanded, her long-lashed eyes glittering like twin cuts of jade. "What's that supposed to mean?"

Dillon studied her mouth. It was swollen from their passionate kisses. He studied her hair. It gleamed gold in the firelight and looked as it should, like she'd just gotten out of bed after rousing lovemaking. He studied her body.

It was as luscious and inviting as a ripe peach just plucked from a tree.

"It means," he warned softly as his eyes lifted seriously to hers. "That I've had a taste of what we could have, Hayley, and I'm not going to let you forget it."

# Chapter Six

"The limo's here."

"So I see." Hayley adjusted the hem of her wedding dress with more than necessary care, avoiding his eyes.

Dillon waited until she had picked up her oversize purse. "Ready?"

"Absolutely." Hayley pushed the words through stiff lips. The sooner she got out of here and away from the scene of the crime, the better, she thought. She still couldn't believe she had done such an impulsive thing. And now she was going to have to live with it. They both were.

"Aren't you forgetting something?"

She turned to see he held her negligee and his silk pajama bottoms in his hands. She flushed bright red. "We could leave them for the owners of the cottage, but they might just think we forgot them and send them back to the neighbors who rented the place."

Which would be even more uncomfortable, Hayley knew. She snatched the garments out of his hands and shoved them into her bag. "You really are incorrigible."

He grinned. "I'm trying," he said.

He fell into step beside her as they started down the

walk. "You don't have to look as though you're headed for the guillotine, you know."

"Right," Hayley countered, rolling her eyes. She hadn't been able to eat a thing this morning. Her nerves were strung tight.

"Hayley—"

"Please, no more conversation, Dillon." Hayley held up her hands in distressed surrender. "Or I really will get a migraine."

Dillon studied her a long moment, then took her at her word.

The ride back to the suburbs was long, tense and silent. Worse, a crowd had gathered in front of the house. "Looks like they're very interested in our wedding night," Dillon murmured, reaching to give her a hand from the limousine.

Hayley took his proffered palm only because she saw no graceful way out of it. "Might as well give them their money's worth," Dillon murmured in her ear as she stepped from the car, then he swept her up into his arms.

Hayley had no choice but to hang on as he strode up the front walk.

"Guess I don't have to ask you how last night went," Marge teased, coming out to stand on the front steps, Christine in her arms.

Dillon swept past his sister, not pausing until he'd carried Hayley over the threshold and delivered another swift, hard, breath-stealing kiss on her lips. "Try to at least look as if you're having fun," he murmured against her mouth.

Slowly he let her down. Hayley's feet touched the floor. To her dismay she was as dizzy and pleasurably disoriented as she had been when they'd made love.

"Mama!" Christine cried, and held out her arms to Hayley.

Hayley reached for her baby, like a drowning sailor reaching for a lifeline. At last, Hayley thought, she'd found the shield she needed to keep Dillon at arm's length. "Hi, darlin'," she crooned, holding her little girl close. "Did you miss Mama?"

Christine hid her face in Hayley's neck and snuggled even closer. Dillon, Hayley noted, looked thoughtful and not as smugly victorious as he had been.

Dillon turned to the neighbors who had gathered to welcome them home. "Hayley and I had a great time. We can't thank you enough."

Knowing it was the least she could do, Hayley seconded his appreciative speech. "Yes. We really..." She choked briefly as she tried to get out the appropriate words. "We had a—a terrific time. It was an enormous surprise. Thank you all."

Dillon winked. "The night clothes were great, too."

Everyone laughed. Hayley blushed.

"Well, guess we better let the newlyweds have their home to themselves," Marge said tactfully. She cast a look at the gutted interior of the home. "Such as it is, anyway."

*I have more than enough to keep me busy now that I'm home again,* Hayley thought, glancing around her at the stripped woodwork and walls, and the half-finished foyer. *And so does Dillon. Once he goes back to work, everything will be fine.*

"I KNOW WHAT you're doing, Hayley. It won't work," Dillon said.

Hayley looked up from the foyer floor. Although they had only been home from their honeymoon for three hours, she had put the time to good use. She'd played with Christine, fed her her lunch and put her down for her nap. Then she'd concentrated on pulling up the rest of the faux marble tile that had covered a beautiful wood floor.

"Sure it will," Hayley retorted. "All I have to do is sand the floor down with the electric sander, then apply a good coat of varnish or maybe wood stain and—"

"I meant the get-up," Dillon said, his hands on his hips. He had changed out of his wedding clothes hours ago, into a navy silk fisherman sweater and tailored khaki slacks.

Beside him, Hayley felt all the more grimy. Not wanting him to know that, she feigned an innocence meant to irritate him and asked coyly, "What get-up?"

Dillon gestured impatiently at her. "The torn, baggy sweatshirt, the loose jeans, the spinster's bun." He sauntered toward her lazily, rested an elbow on the wobbly wooden banister leading up the sweeping staircase. His gaze moved over her slowly, then returned to her eyes.

"If you're trying to impress upon me how unfeminine you can be, forget it," he advised with an amused smile. "I find you even more appealing this way, without artifice of any kind." He sauntered close. "Don't you know your real beauty shines through no matter how you try to hide it?" He reached toward her as if to touch her face.

Hayley swatted at his hand irritably and stepped back over the electric sander. She placed both hands on her hips. "Honestly, Dillon, I think all that champagne you drank yesterday went to your head."

"Something went to my head," he agreed. He hooked an arm about her waist and pulled her close. "But it wasn't champagne, Hayley. It was you."

His warm fragrant breath stirred her hair, reminding her just how thrilling and satisfying his lovemaking had been.

"It was last night."

As much as she wanted to make love with him, she couldn't, wouldn't, sacrifice her dreams. And that meant she couldn't make love with him again. She placed both hands on his chest and shoved. "It was sex."

"That, too," Dillon agreed. He let her go, but kept his eyes on hers.

Hayley hauled in a shaky breath. She could keep him at arm's length, she persuaded herself sternly, all she had to do was try. "And it was a one-night stand," she continued.

Dillon slouched against the wall. He rubbed his handsome jaw contemplatively. "Funny, you didn't strike me as the type who had one-night stands," he drawled, knitting his brows together as if greatly perplexed.

"I don't," Hayley hastened to correct. Then realizing what she had just admitted, said, "Didn't."

He grinned victoriously. "You did."

"Must you keep reminding me of that?" Hayley cried, incensed.

"Someone should."

"Just because I did it once, does not mean I will ever do it again," she said icily.

His blue eyes gleamed wickedly. "So you've informed me."

He looked determined to change her mind about that.

She was just as resolved not to let him.

Hayley picked up her electric sander defiantly and released a loud, put-upon sigh. "Dillon, please. I've got to get this done before Christine wakes up from her nap."

He studied her a long moment. Whatever pleasure he

had felt earlier at being with her was fading fast. "Fine," he said curtly. "I'm going in to the office for a while."

"The one here?"

"The one in the city."

*Good,* Hayley thought.

"I may not be back tonight," he informed her flatly.

Hayley's initial relief faded. If he wasn't, the neighbors would talk. Oh, well, she'd just say he had a hot story to monitor, reporters to assign. It was the nature of his work. They all knew he was a bureau chief for NCN with heavy, ongoing responsibilities.

"Fine," she said cheerfully.

Only it wasn't fine.

Because Dillon didn't come back. Not Sunday evening, not Monday morning, not Monday night. By Tuesday Hayley was deeply depressed. She had wanted to hold him at arm's length and maintain their friendship, not drive him completely out of his home.

It bothered her she cared where he was. It bothered her she missed him. It bothered her she thought about him at all. Heavens, it wasn't as if she was beginning to depend on his presence in her life to make her happy, was it? She knew how dangerous that was. It was like asking to have her heart stomped on!

"This just isn't good," she told Christine as she bathed her that evening. "I'm beginning to get too involved here." She'd lost sight of the fact that this really wasn't her home, but merely an investment property, the sale of which would allow her to purchase her own home, for her and Christine.

"I need to think more about the future," Hayley continued.

"Mama?" Christine giggled, as she splashed Hayley in the face.

Hayley grinned, her spirits already lifting. "Our future."

At midnight she was still working on that future.

DILLON HEARD the rat-a-tat-tat of a manual typewriter the moment he entered the house. Having stayed in the city, he had hoped Hayley would have come to her senses, realized as did he that the powerful attraction between them was something to be savored, not wasted.

His mood tense but hopeful, he followed the sound to the kitchen where Hayley sat, pounding away on the keys. It was an incongruous sight, Hayley in mens flannel pajamas that covered her from head to toe, and white sweat socks. He knew she'd heard him come in. He could tell by the twin spots of color that appeared in her otherwise pale face, but she kept her vision steadfastly glued to the page in front of her.

Dillon didn't know what he'd expected. Recriminations for staying away and not calling to either check on her and the baby or let her know where he was staying. At this point he would take even a coldly uttered greeting. It seemed, however, she was determined to ignore him completely.

"So," Dillon drawled. He sauntered forward across the untiled kitchen floor to stand behind her chair. He was close enough to see the damp hair on the nape of her neck and smell the heady scent of her perfume and know she had recently taken another of her long bubble baths. "What are you up to?"

"Just typing a few letters," Hayley murmured, her tone noncommittal. The pink spots in her cheeks deepened.

"I can see that." Dillon started reading over her shoulder. "Why?"

"I'm still looking for a job, remember? For when I'm done here."

"But that won't be for months."

"Actually, it might happen a little sooner, if I step up the remodeling schedule," Hayley said. She reached for the bottle of correction fluid and, rolling the paper up, dabbed a small amount on an *e* that should have been an *i*.

Dillon felt the first stirrings of panic. He was irritated with Hayley for refusing to admit they were extremely sexually compatible, but he hadn't wanted this. "How soon?" he asked, his tone clipped.

Hayley shrugged a slender shoulder. "I don't know. A couple of months. It could happen even more quickly if I subbed out a lot of the interior work." She looked around her thoughtfully at the stripped walls and half-painted kitchen cabinets. "But of course that would cut into my profits quite a bit. Labor is expensive." Her pretty mouth pursed. "It's a definite trade-off."

"I'd think the more profits you can reap out of this place, the better," Dillon said, wishing he didn't recall quite so accurately how sweet that bare mouth of hers tasted, or just how well she could kiss. "For your future," he amended hastily, when he saw she was about to take offense.

"Yes, but the question is at what cost ultimately," Hayley said, giving him a pointed look.

Dillon was quiet. He knew he'd deserved that. He had put too much pressure on her, but damn it, what was he supposed to do? They'd taken their relationship a giant step forward, making love the way they had. Now she wanted to forget all about it, pretend it hadn't happened, and he wasn't sure he could do that. He knew he didn't want to. He also knew she wasn't giving him much choice.

He'd either have to try like hell to be more patient with her and hope, given time, she would come around, or lose her entirely. The one thing they wouldn't do, he decided firmly, was talk about it anymore. They had done that enough as it was, to bitter result.

He glanced at the stack of envelopes next to her desk. All had labels. All were empty. "Why aren't you using my computer?" he asked, focusing for a minute on the practical, instead of the highly improbable and romantic.

Hayley shrugged again, the movement jiggling her breasts enough to tell him she wasn't wearing a bra. "You weren't here," she said, while Dillon struggled to contain both a groan and the rising heat in his groin. Her eyes focused on his as she continued in the same matter-of-fact tone, "I couldn't ask you if it was okay."

Dillon had the distinct feeling even if he had been there Hayley would have died rather than ask him for any favors. "You could have called me at the office," he pointed out reasonably.

"How was I supposed to know you were there?"

*Ouch,* Dillon thought.

Hayley got up and pushed her chair with a screech. "Look, you don't own me," she said impatiently. "I don't own you. We may be married—in name only—it doesn't mean we suddenly have to ask permission from each other to breathe."

"Is that how it was in your first marriage?" Dillon asked. He pulled out a chair, turned it around and sank into it, placing his arm over the back.

"No!" Hayley looked stunned. "Hank and I each went our separate ways."

"So much so that you didn't mind him going overseas?"

"Now, *that* I didn't say," Hayley corrected as she tore out the first letter and rolled another sheet of clean paper into her typewriter. "I did mind him being out of the country for months on end, especially during the war. I worried he might get hurt."

Realizing all over again what he'd neglected to tell her—that he'd not only recruited Hank personally, but had been the person who'd sent him out on the assignment during which he'd been killed, Dillon lowered his gaze to the tabletop.

He should have been straight with her from the first, he thought. But looking back on it, he didn't really see how he could have been, not when she'd regarded him so suspiciously from the outset. No, it was better to let sleeping issues lie. Besides, what happened then was over. It wasn't as if it could be undone, even if he did tell her.

He wished he could keep his mouth shut, but he was curious about Hayley. "What about when Hank was in-country?" he asked. *What had their relationship been like then?* "You were married to him about a year before he left, weren't you?"

Hayley nodded. "Yes, but we weren't joined at the hip. We continued to lead our own lives and pursue our own careers."

"You were still working as a financial analyst then, weren't you?"

Hayley rested her elbows on the typewriter. "And he was trying to make it happen for him as a reporter. When he got hired by NCN, it was like a dream come true for him."

"Did you know you were pregnant when he accepted the job covering Desert Storm?"

"Yes."

"And you encouraged him to go?" Dillon marveled at her independence even though a part of him really couldn't understand. Most new husbands and wives wanted their partners with them, period. That went double when they were expecting the birth of their first child. But to his surprise, Hayley seemed to have no such feelings.

"Of course I encouraged him to go."

"But?" Dillon prodded, sensing there was more.

"We had an agreement he would come home as often as possible once the baby was born."

"Most wives wouldn't have been that understanding."

Hayley bit her lip. Some of the color left her cheeks. "To tell you the truth, I didn't want him here every day, especially when I made the decision to stop working."

He faced her incredulously. "Why not?"

Hayley shrugged and avoided his eyes. "If he had been here, I might have started depending on him." She swallowed hard and took a deep breath. Their eyes met. "I've seen it happen, Dillon," she continued earnestly. "Capable career women, who've turned into clinging vines when they're home with a child for any length of time. I never wanted that."

Or in other words, Dillon thought, Hayley had married with one foot out the door. That explained why she had adapted to widowhood so well and why she hadn't minded being married to a man in such a dangerous profession.

"And that's also why I'm working on my résumés tonight," Hayley continued pragmatically. "Now that I've done a number of paintings to show my skill, I need to start the process of setting up interviews with publishing houses. It'll take a while for me to find free-lance work,

I know, especially since I have no former experience in the field, but I'm determined to succeed.''

And succeed she would, Dillon thought. "I don't know how much help I can be," he offered genially, "but I do have a few contacts—"

Hayley cut him off. "No. Thanks." For her the subject was closed.

Realizing how little she would allow herself to take from him, Dillon felt guiltier than ever. "At least use my computer," he urged as she began to type on the hopelessly outdated manual typewriter again. "You can type your query letters in half the time."

Hayley paused, clearly tempted. "You wouldn't mind?"

"Not at all."

She studied him, silently assessing, deciding, Dillon figured, if she could trust him again. He wanted her to feel she could. "Hayley," he said, resisting the urge to cover her hand with his only because he was afraid that at this point she might take any physical touch the wrong way. "I'm sorry. Sorry we fought."

"So am I. I don't like fighting."

Dillon's heart was pounding. He wanted to take her in his arms, cement their conciliatory words with a hug. He knew he couldn't, not without being tempted to do more than simply hold her. So he sat where he was. "Truce?"

"That depends," she said slowly, her green eyes lighting up suspiciously again, "on just what it is that you want from me."

Dillon had had a lot of time to think about that when he was closeted up in a hotel room in New York. "To know we can count on each other through thick or thin, as friends."

"I don't know, Dillon."

"Why not?"

She fidgeted restlessly in her chair. "What you're describing sounds far more intimate than what I had in mind."

Dillon grinned. She was weakening, he could see it. "Hey, I didn't include sex," he teased, pretending to be offended.

Hayley smirked and rolled her eyes. "As if you would get that demand met," she retorted dryly.

They grinned at each other, the sexy banter lightening the tension between them. "Come on, Hayley," Dillon persuaded, liking it when she looked at him like that, her eyes all soft and full of a very tenuous trust. "Give it a try."

Hayley sat all the way back in her chair. It was so hard to be around Dillon, even now, nearly seventy-two hours after they'd made love. Just looking at him, she recalled the womanly way he'd made her feel. If only they were more alike. Or wanted the same things out of life. But they didn't, she reminded herself firmly. And she had a future to ensure for herself and her daughter. There was only one way that could be accomplished. To manage that, she had to keep Dillon at arm's length.

She planted both hands on her slender hips and studied him sternly as she spelled out the terms for her continued employment. "You promise you'll keep your hands to yourself?" she demanded archly.

Dillon had always prided himself on being a man of his word. She'd already tempted him to break that promise once. "I promise I'll try," he said.

Hayley shook her head, the slight movement of her body jiggling her breasts beneath the opaque forest green and navy plaid pajama top. "Not good enough, Dillon," she chided.

"Okay, okay." Dillon told himself he was not thinking about making love to her again. "I promise."

She stared at him, assessing him another long moment, then finally capitulated, as Dillon had hoped she would. "All right," she said slowly. "I'll accommodate you as long as you accommodate me."

"And if one of us fails?"

"Depends." Hayley lifted her shoulders, then let them fall. "If it's you trying to get me into bed again," Hayley continued, "all bets are off. If it's in the other area, of us counting on one another and we screw up, then…" Her eyes lifted to his and held a moment. "I guess we try again," she said, her expression determined. "Try and make this buddy system of ours work," she finished, her low voice once again taking on a practical edge.

Dillon knew how hard this was going to be for her. She didn't know how to let herself count on someone else. "Okay, you've got a deal," he said.

He watched her gather up her papers. "Want me to show you how to use my computer?" he offered.

Hayley's head lifted. Moments earlier her gaze had been intimate. Now her look was as impersonal as her cool tone. "It's an IBM, right?"

Dillon nodded, trying not to feel too disappointed. "Right."

"What kind of software are you using?"

"WordPerfect."

"There's no need. I'm already familiar with it."

Silently Dillon watched her gather her things and head to his study. Once again she didn't seem to need him. She didn't seem to need anyone. He wondered if she ever would.

# Chapter Seven

Dillon had just stepped out of the shower when he heard the baby crying. He wrapped a towel around his middle and stuck his head out his bedroom door. "Hayley?" he yelled.

There was no answer.

Down the hall he could still hear Christine crying as if her heart would break. Afraid now that something was terribly wrong, Dillon dashed down the hall and rushed into Christine's room.

She was standing in her crib, her eyes red rimmed, her plump little face covered with tears. When she saw him, dripping wet and clad only in a towel, she only cried harder. "Now, now," Dillon soothed her awkwardly. He glanced over his shoulder, into the adjoining bath. No Hayley.

In her crib, Christine wailed louder. If there was anything Dillon hated it was a crying kid. Sensing the only way to quiet her was to pick her up, he lifted her out of her crib. "Hey, hey," he said, patting her awkwardly on the back. "Stop crying now. I don't know where your mother is, but she's got to be around here somewhere."

Christine sniffed and took a shuddering breath. She

rested her damp face on his shoulder. "Mama," she whispered.

"I know exactly how you feel," Dillon soothed. "I'd like to know where she is, too."

"I'm right here," Hayley said breathlessly from somewhere behind them.

Dillon turned, Christine cradled in his arms.

Hayley's glance swept his wet form, skimming over his damp skin, slicked-back hair, and the thick terrycloth towel knotted at his waist and hanging to his knees. She turned her astonished glance back to his face. "What's going on?" she demanded. "Why's Christine crying? Dillon?"

"That's what I'd like to know," he countered gruffly. He handed Christine over to her mother and nearly lost his towel in the process. He grabbed it just in time, embarrassed to find himself feeling aroused, simply from being close to Hayley when he was nearly naked. Not that it took being nearly naked for him to respond to her. All he had to do was be within three feet of her, in the same room with her. All he had to do was think about their wedding night.

Damn it all, nothing was helping. And he wished Hayley would stop breathing that way, as if she was permanently excited. He wished she would stop looking at him like she was remembering their wedding night, too.

Tucking the towel in firmly at his waist, Dillon turned his aggravation back to the reason for their current predicament and his nearly naked state. "Where were you? Christine was crying her head off when I got out of the shower."

"I had to run next door. Dillon, she's wet!"

Dillon stiffened at the accusatory note underlying Hayley's equally agitated voice. "Of course she's wet," he grumbled.

"You didn't change her?"

"I don't know how to change her!"

"Off!" Christine said, pushing at her pajama bottoms even before Hayley laid her on the changing table.

"Well, then it's time you learned," Hayley grumbled irritably.

"Why?" Dillon regarded her cantankerously. "I don't have kids."

"You might someday."

"Doubtful."

"Okay." Hayley gave up. "Don't learn."

"No, you're right," he amended quickly. "I need to learn."

"Why, if you're not going to have kids?"

"Christine," Dillon said shortly, wishing Hayley didn't look so darn fresh and pretty first thing every morning. "She might need another diaper change someday—"

"If she does, I'll do it." Hayley cut him off brusquely.

"Back to that again?"

"She isn't your responsibility, Dillon." Deftly Hayley stripped Christine of her wet pajama pants and diaper, reached for a dry one, and slid it beneath her. Interested now and determined to learn, maybe because she didn't seem to want him to, Dillon watched Hayley sprinkle baby powder lightly over Christine's bottom.

Christine held out a hand toward Dillon and smiled, beckoning him to approach. Smiling back, he let her take his index finger, and curl her tiny palm around it.

Hayley pulled two edges of the cloth diaper over Christine's hip and reached for the diaper pin with the yellow duck on the head of it. "Why are you sliding your hand beneath the diaper?" Dillon asked.

"So that if I stick anyone with this pin, I stick myself."

"Let me try the other side," Dillon said.

She cast him an astonished look. There was no denying, by the damp state of Dillon's skin and hair and the towel knotted around his waist, that he'd wasted no time in coming to her baby's rescue. Nor was there any denying the way her pulse speeded up dangerously at just the sight of him, so sexily attired.

The wariness in her green eyes and the way she stepped back suddenly cut him to the quick. "Don't think I can do it?" Dillon taunted.

"Not sure why you'd want to," Hayley corrected, lifting her chin. "Besides, isn't this a parent's work?"

Did he really come off as that selfish and self-involved? Dillon tried not to notice just how much her veiled jab at his character, or lack of it in her estimation, stung. "Just let me have a go at it," he said.

"Be my guest." Hayley glided aside with a welcoming sweep of her slender arm.

Dillon stepped in beside her. There was nothing to this. He'd just seen Hayley do it. He grabbed the edges of the diaper, slid his hand inside the cloth, the way he'd seen Hayley do it, and inserted the pin. Easy as one two three he clasped it. "Voilà!" he said, lifting both hands in triumph.

Christine giggled and kicked. Hayley laughed, too. Dillon looked down. The diaper pin was in the diaper all right. It just wasn't holding it together.

"You only got the pin through one side of the diaper," Hayley said.

Dillon stubbornly tried again. This time he managed to get the diaper edges pinned together. Only problem was, when he lifted Christine up, to a standing position, the diaper slid cockeyed down one hip.

He turned to Hayley who was fighting not to smile. "Too loose?"

"Just a bit." She studied his face and sighed loudly. "I suppose you want to try again?"

By now it was a matter of pride. His pride. "You know what they say," Dillon muttered, trying hard to keep the grim determination out of his voice. "The third time's the charm." It was no wonder he'd never been inclined to have kids.

"Hurrah for Dillon!" Hayley led the applause after this third attempt. "He did it."

Christine clapped awkwardly, her tiny face lighting up with radiant happiness. "Dillon!" she said.

"Did you hear that, Dillon?" Hayley turned toward him excitedly. "She said your name!"

He was embarrassed at the surge of emotion welling up inside him. Much more of this and he'd be acting as idiotic as a parent. "Yeah, I heard it," he growled, embarrassed. "Why did you go out, anyway?"

Hayley took Christine and headed downstairs for the kitchen. "I went next door to Carol's, to borrow some milk for Christine's breakfast."

Dillon grabbed his robe and followed. "You should have told me," he said. "I would have gone to the store for you."

Hayley shrugged off his offer without looking him directly in the face. "I didn't want to impose."

"Then you could have borrowed my Blazer," Dillon persisted, determined to get her to depend on him just a little bit, whether she wanted to or not.

"No," Hayley said firmly.

Dillon followed her around the kitchen, from refrigerator to cabinet to stove. "Why not?"

"Because it's a standard."

"So?" He watched her add milk to Christine's plastic drinking cup.

Hayley snapped on the spill-proof top with more than necessary force. "So I don't know how to drive a standard."

"So I'll teach you."

"No." With a smile for her daughter, Hayley handed Christine her milk and settled her in the high chair.

Dillon continued to follow her around. "It's not hard, Hayley," he said. "You have a license, don't you?"

"Yes." Hayley turned to face him, her arms crossed at her waist. "But I don't have any insurance."

"So? You're my wife. I'll add you to my policy."

Hayley's chin pushed out stubbornly and stayed there.

"I'm only being practical," Dillon persisted, ignoring her mutinous expression. "The easier it is for you to get around, the sooner the house'll get done. The sooner we'll both be free."

Hayley froze. So did Dillon. He hadn't meant to say that. He hadn't figured it would hurt him so much to think about it, either.

"Besides, it'll be more economical this way," he continued.

Hayley took a deep breath. She focused on the sun shining through the bay windows. "I see your point," she said slowly. "It would be more convenient. And this way I wouldn't have to depend so on the neighbors."

Back to that again. Her damnable independence! Still, she had agreed to take driving lessons from him. It was a start.

"Don't look so petrified," Dillon said. "It'll be a piece of cake."

A PIECE OF CAKE was not exactly how Hayley would have termed it. "I feel like I should be wearing a sign around my neck. Get in the Car With This Woman at Your Own Risk.''

Dillon felt a stab of panic. He loved this Blazer. It was the first and only thing he had rushed out to buy for himself when he'd returned to the States. Practical enough to be good in the snow, or take off-road, if the mood struck him, yet good enough on gas and insurance to be economical, it was his baby. He hated the idea of anything happening to it almost as much as he hated the idea of anything happening to Hayley or Christine.

"Surely you jest," he said.

"Not really."

Hayley didn't look like she was kidding, Dillon noted nervously.

"Did I tell you one of my cousins tried to teach me how to drive his sports car once? We spent thirty minutes in a parking lot and I was never able to get it out of gear."

"So you had a bad teacher." Dillon shrugged it off. "Put the key in the ignition."

Hayley rolled her eyes. "It's already in the ignition," she pointed out dryly.

"See?" Dillon teased. "You're already one step ahead of me."

She shot him a sexy smile. "You're humoring me."

"And you're stalling."

Hayley closed her eyes, gripped the steering wheel tightly with both hands and repeated stalwartly, "I think I can, I think I can, I think I can."

"Ah, *The Little Engine That Could.*"

Hayley bowed her head over the steering wheel and seemed to concentrate even harder. Or maybe she was praying. Dillon couldn't tell.

"Positive thinking works," she murmured.

It sure did something, Dillon thought wryly.

He and Hayley had only been out in this parking lot for five minutes and already his mind was filled with licentious thoughts. Maybe it was the scent of perfume or the fall of her silky hair across her shoulders. Maybe it was just the thought that they were in a parked car alone at night or the fact that he was attempting to teach her how to drive a standard transmission that was making him feel like they were a couple of kids. But right now all he wanted to do was take her parking. Haul her across the gearshift and into his arms, and simply kiss her and hold her for hours on end. And that was crazy, considering how old he was and considering the promise he had made. A promise he had sworn to himself he wouldn't break unless she wanted to break it first.

"Ready?"

She opened her eyes slowly and sent him a baleful look. He chuckled.

"What's so funny?" she demanded, straightening so rigidly she unwittingly thrust out her breasts.

Dillon shrugged and returned his eyes to her face. "I've just never seen you look so out of your element, that's all." Except for their wedding night.

"Yeah, well, commit the scene to memory because I doubt like hell you'll ever see me look this way again," she grumbled irritably as she shoved her hair out of her face.

"Don't like not knowing how to do something, huh?" he teased.

"No, I don't," Hayley said.

Looking at her, Dillon thought about the promise he had made and cursed himself for ever making it. "There's only one way to remedy this. Let's get started. Okay, put your left foot on the clutch. The gearshift in first." Because she was gripping the gearshift too tentatively, he cupped his hand over hers, held it down firmly. "Give it a little bit of gas. Ease up on the clutch until it starts going forward. And once it starts picking up speed—"

"How fast?" she asked, sounding panicked again.

"Fifteen or twenty miles an hour, then put it into second. Ease up on the gas as you shift gears, Hayley. That's it. That's it," Dillon praised.

To their mutual relief, driving his Blazer proved a lot easier for Hayley than she had suspected. They tooled aimlessly around the parking lot for the next couple of minutes, cruising along about twenty-five miles an hour. To Dillon's increasing delight, Hayley looked like a kid who'd just discovered how to ride a bike. "I like the way your Blazer handles," she said admiringly.

*I like the way you handle,* Dillon thought as her slim foot worked the gas pedal.

"How do we stop?"

*That's the problem,* he thought, *if we started I don't think I could stop. You, either.* As they had aptly proved to each other on their wedding night.

"Dillon?" Hayley practically shouted. "How do we stop?"

Dillon jerked back to the present. "Uh, sorry, Hay— Christ! Watch out for that light standard!"

"I see it," Hayley informed him irascibly.

"As you start slowing, you downshift. Yeah, put your foot on the clutch, push it in, shift it down to first, now brake."

The Blazer halted successfully, with a bit of a lurch.

"See, that wasn't so hard, was it?" Dillon studied her face, the flush of pride in her cheeks and the excited glitter in her eyes. "Want to try it again and take it up to third this time?" he asked.

"Okay."

Hayley pushed in the clutch, gave it a little gas, and they were off, moving from first to second, second to third, and finally when she reached a cruising speed of thirty-five by avoiding the strategically placed speed bumps, into fourth.

"This is fun!" she exclaimed excitedly.

Not as much as watching her drive, Dillon thought dreamily.

"Damn!" Hayley swore, a knife-edge of panic in her voice. "Another car! What do I do? What do I do?" she cried, as it continued to come straight for them.

Dillon didn't know whether the teenagers saw them and were playing chicken with them or weren't paying attention. He did know a wreck was imminent unless Hayley did something. "Downshift and brake."

Hayley downshifted all right, but she forgot the most important part. The gears ground with earsplitting imprecision, tearing the living daylights out of his transmission. The Blazer rocked and swerved, then lurched to a halt in the nick of time. Dillon was still swearing as the car full of teenagers honked and passed, then burned rubber as they left the parking lot and sped away. "You forgot to put in the clutch," Dillon said.

"I know," Hayley said. "I'm sorry. See, that's the problem." She tugged off her gloves and threw them against the dash.

"What?" Dillon asked, as mesmerized by her display of temper as he was by her beauty.

"When something like that—something I haven't meticulously planned for—comes up I panic." Just like she had panicked right after she and Dillon had made love! She recalled how she had acted then and since. Like a confused, lovestruck teen who didn't know what she wanted—only that she was miserable.

"You'll get the hang of it," Dillon soothed.

Of driving. Yes. But relationships? That was something else entirely. "Maybe in a zillion years," she retorted. She pivoted toward him. Tears of frustration that had little to do with her driving and everything to do with their personal situation, burned hotly in her eyes. "Oh, Dillon, who are we kidding?" Hayley cut the engine abruptly, and pushed miserably from the car. "I can't do this."

She'd thought the two of them could be just friends. But she was beginning to see that was going to be much harder than she'd thought. Every time she was around him, she was reminded how good it had been between them. And then she would start wanting and yes, even needing him, all over again. And she knew what a trap that was! Because if she let herself need Dillon and then he walked away from her at year's end, as planned, she would be devastated.

Dillon got out and strode after her. "Yes, you can do it."

He put his hands on her shoulders, tried to turn her in the direction of the Blazer. Feet planted firmly apart on the pavement, she refused to budge. She didn't want to sit next to him in the Blazer again, didn't want to be even that close. "I can't. I tried."

"So you'll try again," Dillon reasoned pleasantly.

Hayley thought about making love with him again and how hard, if not damn nigh impossible, it would be to walk away from him a second time. She shrugged free of him. "No."

Dillon strode after her, caught her by the back of the coat and turned her around again. "Why not?"

"Because I might wreck your car," she said. *And you might wreck my life.*

He pointed to his chest. "Do I look worried?"

"No," she retorted wryly, slowly regaining her sense of humor as they began to banter back and forth. With effort she forced her mind back to her driving lesson. "Which doesn't say much for you, 'cause only a fool wouldn't be worried with me behind the wheel of a standard transmission."

"You're selling yourself short."

"No, I'm not." Hayley disagreed with a weary deliberation that seemed to cut clear to her soul. "I know all about things that are loaned out, friend to friend, relative to relative, remember? And I'm just being practical. If I were to drive your Blazer and something happened to it, you'd hate me."

Looking down at her frustrated expression in the glow of the parking lot lights, Dillon knew she couldn't have been more wrong. He loved every inch of her. "No, I wouldn't," he said calmly, wondering if there was something else on her mind, too, something she wasn't telling him.

"Yes, you would," Hayley disagreed. "You'd resent me. You'd rue the day you ever let me move into your home, never mind married me."

The only thing he rued, Dillon thought sagely, was not being able to make love with her. And that was what they had done, not "have sex," as she had asserted, but made love. "I'm not one of your relatives, Hayley," he said flatly, meaning it. His eyes burned into hers. "I'm not going to think of you as a burden to me."

"You say that now," Hayley said on a tremulous sigh.

"I say that always," Dillon disagreed. He lifted her face to his and continued gently, "You won't be a burden for me. Ever. But—'' he grinned suddenly, seeing a way he could profit from this, too ''—if you're worried about putting me to the trouble of teaching you to drive, there is something you could do for me.''

She wished she could think about something besides kissing him whenever they were this close. ''Yeah, like what?'' Not making love again, she hoped!

Dillon let out a breath. ''You could help me do something nice for my sister.''

For a moment Hayley looked taken aback, as if she had expected him to ask for something more personal from her. ''Marge?'' she croaked.

Dillon nodded. ''Her forty-fifth birthday is coming up, a week from Saturday. I've missed about the last twenty of her birthdays, 'cause I've always been overseas. Since I'm around this year, I want to give her a surprise party.'' He hesitated briefly, not sure how Hayley would take the next. ''I've already talked to all her kids. They're all coming home from college for the weekend. But in order for it to be a surprise, they'll need somewhere to stay. I was hoping they could stay with us. Just for Friday night,'' he amended hastily. ''I'm sure Marge will want them home with her on Saturday.''

''Well, sure,'' Hayley said. ''That is, if you think they wouldn't mind all the renovations going on.''

''Are you kidding? These are college kids. They've assured me all they need is a sleeping bag and a place to shower.''

''We can do better than that,'' Hayley said. ''We've still got the two double beds that belonged to the other owners. We can put your two nieces in one room, your nephew in the other. It should work fine.''

Dillon smiled, relieved. ''I was hoping you'd say that.''

They grinned at each other.

He thought about kissing her. He had the feeling she was thinking the same.

His mouth set grimly, he took her elbow and headed in the direction of the Blazer. "Back to the driving lesson," he said.

Hayley groaned and put her face in her hands. "Dillon—" she moaned.

Dillon knew if they didn't get started now he would forget the promises he'd made and start something she would love tonight and hate him for tomorrow. He yanked open the driver's door and gave her a lift up. "Behind the wheel, Hayley," he ordered sternly. "Right now."

She'd successfully gotten herself out of lovemaking; she wasn't getting herself out of this.

# Chapter Eight

"I understand why you waited so long to get married, Uncle Dillon," Dillon's nephew Andy said Friday evening as the six of them sat down at the dinner table. "Hayley's a fox!"

Dillon cast an amused look at Hayley. "I quite agree."

"Well, I didn't think Uncle Dillon was ever going to get married," Cara admitted, as she passed a steaming bowl of fettucine to her younger sister Vickie. "Especially after what happened last time!"

"What last time?" Hayley asked.

"You mean Uncle Dillon didn't tell you?" Cara gasped. "Why, he practically got left at the altar."

"You mean he left his fiancée at the altar," Vickie corrected. "Isn't that right, Uncle Dillon?"

"It was a mutual decision," Dillon said as he helped himself to a serving of Hayley's chicken parmesan. "And I really doubt Hayley's interested in my past love life."

"Wrong," Hayley said. She cast Dillon an amused glance. "I'm very interested. Keep talking, girls."

"Well, you should have seen her, Aunt Hayley—"

"She was beautiful—"

"A reporter—"

"Everyone thought they were a perfect match."

"So what happened?" Hayley looked at Dillon. He wasn't squirming in his seat, but she could tell by the excessively passive expression on his face that he wanted to.

"I know what happened," Andy speculated. "Uncle Dillon got cold feet."

Hayley grinned at Dillon, enjoying his discomfiture immensely for some reason that she couldn't begin to fathom. Maybe because he'd been so nosy about the most intimate details of her life. "Did you get cold feet?" she asked Dillon.

"Uh," Dillon tugged at his collar as if it was choking him. "We both did. Andy, would you pass the salad, please? And let's all talk about something else."

"Okay, how come you and Hayley didn't have a big wedding?" Cara asked.

Dillon looked at Hayley, giving her a chance to answer first. "I didn't want one," she said quietly, knowing it was the absolute truth.

"Why not?" Cara persisted.

Hayley shrugged.

"Did you have one before?" Vickie asked.

"No. I didn't want one then, either. It seemed like a lot of fuss." *For something that might not even last,* Hayley thought. Then, as now, she had little faith in the kindness of fate, at least where she was concerned. Not to mention the fact she hadn't had anyone to help her foot the bill or give her away.

"If you ask me, I think they were just in a hurry to get married," Andy teased. "I think Dillon was so hot for her that—"

"Andy!" Both girls cried in unison.

"Don't worry." Andy soothed Dillon above the protests of his sisters. "We understand the two of you are still in the honeymoon phase. We'll go to bed early and we won't bother you. The two of you can make all the noise you want.''

Hayley turned beet red despite herself.

"Thanks, Andy," Dillon said dryly, "that's very sporting of you."

"So where are we sleeping?" Cara asked.

Hayley smiled, glad the subject had been changed to something safer. "There are two spare bedrooms upstairs. I thought I'd put you girls in one bedroom and Andy in the other," she said.

"No way," Vickie said. "Cara snores and she kicks!"

"I do not!"

"Do so. I'm taking a sofa."

"That's not necessary," Dillon said, without blinking an eye. "You can have the bed in Christine's room."

Hayley choked on her wine. Dillon knew she had put Christine's crib in the sitting room of her master suite. Everyone turned to her in unison as she caught her breath. Hand to her throat, she wheezed, "Dillon, that's not such a good idea. Christine's had a cold," she fibbed, seeking an explanation that would satisfy the kids and get her out of this predicament. "I had planned on staying in there with her tonight."

Cara's brow furrowed. "She looks fine to me."

"I know, but sometimes she coughs in the night," Hayley continued, adding to her fib.

"Then I'll get up with her," Vickie volunteered cheerfully. "I don't mind. Honestly, Aunt Hayley, I love kids."

"Yeah, and this way Dillon and Hayley get some time to themselves." Andy winked at them both lecherously.

Dillon grinned at Hayley speculatively. "Looks like it's all settled," he drawled.

Settled indeed!

"I DON'T SEE what the big deal is," Dillon began the moment they were alone.

Hayley whirled on him furiously. "Don't you?"

"No. Where'd you think you were going to sleep tonight?"

"Where I always sleep. In with Christine."

"Will you keep your voice down?" He guided her farther away from his bedroom door. "Someone will hear."

Hayley had changed into her own pajamas before letting him in. "I don't care."

He clapped a hand over her mouth. "Well, I do. I've already been humiliated once in the marriage department, in front of my family. I don't need to be humiliated again. Face it, Hayley. We perpetuated this lie, now we're going to have to live with it."

"That doesn't mean we have to sleep together," she persisted.

"When we have guests we do," Dillon argued. He walked into his closet and came out with a pair of pajama pants in his hand. His dark brow quirked as he looked at her. "Unless you *want* the kids to figure out what's really going on here."

"There's no way they could know about our arrangement," she whispered back stubbornly.

"Maybe not precisely," Dillon pointed out calmly as he shucked his pants in front of her. Seeing he was about to dispense with his shorts, too, Hayley hastily turned away from him. She didn't want to see him in all his male glory, or be reminded how it had felt to have him deep inside her.

"But all it'd take is one mention to Marge that you and I aren't sharing the same bed," Dillon continued as he trod closer and whispered over her shoulder, in her ear. "And Marge would wonder about it and eventually tell

Carol she was worried about me and why. And then Carol would—''

Hayley lifted her hands in surrender and pivoted to face him. ''Okay, okay. I get your drift,'' she mumbled. Dillon stripped off his shirt as casually as he had just changed into his pajama pants. She tore her eyes from the curling tufts of hair on his muscular chest.

As much as she hated to admit it, Dillon was right about this. They didn't need anyone else nosing in their private affairs. That was what had prompted this whole marriage business in the first place. She glanced up to find him studying her. ''And you do not have to look so pleased about this!'' she continued cantankerously, wishing he'd chosen to wear something other than the paisley silk pajama pants the neighbors had given him as a wedding present.

''How else do you expect me to look? I've got a beautiful woman sleeping in my bed—''

''I'm not beautiful!''

''The hell you're not!''

She flushed with pleasure. He really seemed to think so. When he looked at her like that, he made her feel beautiful. And that, too, was dangerous. She went to the closet and brought out the spare blanket he kept on the shelf.

''Now what are you doing?'' Dillon asked.

Hayley whipped back the covers on his bed, rolled the spare blanket into a thick line and tried not to think about the quivers generating in her tummy. ''I'm putting a blanket down the middle to keep us apart,'' she said, as she patted it into place.

As she continued to bend over, she imagined she felt his gaze rest hotly on her hips and thighs. The tingles in her tummy arrowed even lower. Hayley straightened, a flush of increased awareness on her face.

"If I really wanted to be next to you," he pointed out amicably with a grin that said when so moved he dared anything, "that blanket would be no barrier, Hayley."

She crossed her arms defiantly beneath her breasts and told herself not to look at his bare chest, or recall how good that mat of hair and wall of firmly muscled skin had felt against her. "It stays, just the same," she announced sternly.

He watched her slip beneath the covers. "No nightie?" he asked, disappointed.

Hayley glanced down at her own mismatched sweat clothes and thick white crew socks. Not coincidentally the outfit was the most unerotic thing she owned. "Sorry, loverboy," she said sweetly. "I'm sleeping as is."

"Damn." He walked toward his side of the king-size bed, his pajama pants riding low on his lean hips. To Hayley's dismay they looked like they might slip even lower at any second.

"I was remembering that white, lacy number. You know, the one you wore on our honeymoon..."

Forcing her eyes back to Dillon's face, Hayley said stiffly, "I haven't forgotten it." Nor had she forgotten what had happened when he began intimately exploring what was beneath the wispy layer of chiffon and lace.

"Good. I haven't, either," Dillon said. "I enjoyed seeing you in it."

Unfortunately for Hayley, it had been a very sexy experience being seen in the gown, feeling Dillon's eyes move sensually over her from head to toe, eliciting flames of desire everywhere he gazed. It was the inevitable complications that had developed later, after they'd made love and recovered their usual good sense, that she detested recalling. Deciding it would be best if he were *fully* clothed, she snapped, "Where's your pajama top?"

"Why?" He slid in beside her, on his side of the rolled-up blanket. He propped himself up on his elbow and surveyed her with a guileless grin. "Do you want to borrow it?"

"No," Hayley said with exaggerated patience, "I want you to wear it, Dillon."

He rolled over onto his back and clasped both hands behind his head. The action only served to show her how flat his stomach and how well-endowed the rest of him was. "Sorry, no can do," Dillon said, sounding even more chipper, to Hayley's increasing aggravation.

"Why not?" she demanded, gulping hard around the sudden dryness in her throat.

"'Cause I can't sleep if I'm hot," Dillon explained without apology. "And if I can't sleep..."

Hayley recalled all too well what had happened the last night they hadn't been able to sleep. She glared at him, letting him know with a single look that would not happen again. "Stay on your own side of the bed," she warned.

He lifted the sheet to his chin and feigned a comical concern for his virtue. Arching his brow he warned with mock solemnity, "You stay on yours."

She sent him another withering look. He merely smiled at her and switched off the light. Feeling even more disgruntled, Hayley rolled onto her side. She turned on her right side, then on her left, then lay on her back staring up at the ceiling. All ways felt equally uncomfortable. Worse, she knew she would never be able to sleep dressed as she was. It wasn't her sweats that were bothering her, but her bra. She never slept in one, and right now the lacy strip of cloth felt very confining.

Beside her Dillon shifted around restlessly. "My sheets are cold," he complained. "Are yours?"

"Not as cold as if I'd gotten into bed without my shirt," she said in a deadpan tone.

His low laughter filled the darkness. It was a very sexy, provocative sound.

Hayley continued to stare at the ceiling, wishing her mind weren't filled with wistful thoughts of making love to him. "Dillon?"

"Hmm?" he replied softly.

"What the kids said, about you being engaged." *About me being so beautiful, the perfect match for you.* "Is that true?"

"Why do you ask?"

She rolled toward him. His profile was bathed in silvery moonlight, making him look even more handsome. "I'm curious, that's all," she fibbed.

"Yeah, well—" He slanted her an aggrieved glance. "Curiosity killed the cat."

"Or in other words it's none of my business."

Silence fell between them once again.

"It's not easy to talk about." Dillon paused again and folded his hands behind his head. "It's embarrassing."

"Why?"

He sighed and continued to stare at the ceiling. "Because I was so stupid." He let out a soft, ragged sigh. "I thought she loved me, really loved me, when all she really felt was gratitude." He rolled onto his side, so he was facing Hayley again, and worked his palm over the rolled up blanket, smoothing it unnecessarily. "I was her boss. I hired her right out of graduate school. I taught her how to survive in the field, how to cultivate sources and dig incessantly until you get the story you set out to get. We were together a lot. And somehow the work camaraderie blossomed into an affair. She wanted marriage—''

''You didn't?'' Hayley interrupted.

Dillon shrugged indifferently and lifted his eyes to hers. ''Not really. But she did. So we leapt ahead with our plans. And it wasn't until we came back to the States a week before the wedding that everything blew up in our faces.''

''What happened?''

Again Dillon was silent for a long time. His palm continued to smooth the blanket gently, methodically, in the same way he had once caressed her skin. Hayley flushed.

''She met up with one of her older brother's friends, a guy she used to date in high school. He was also a close family friend. He was going to be one of the ushers.''

He didn't say anything else, but Hayley could guess the rest. ''She left you for him?'' Hayley asked incredulously. That was impossible. No man was sexier or more attractive than Dillon.

Dillon got up to get a drink of water. He brought the glass back to the bed and lounged on top of the covers, his back propped against the headboard, one leg raised and bent at the knee. ''It wasn't quite that cut-and-dried, but yeah, that's the gist of it.''

''Why?'' Hayley looked deep into his dark blue eyes and just couldn't imagine it.

Dillon took another long drink of water and swallowed slowly. ''She realized she loved him. What she felt for me—'' Dillon grimaced. Water beaded on his lower lip. He wiped it off with the back of his left hand, then handed his glass to her. ''Was gratitude, for all I'd done.''

Hayley took a sip of the water and returned the glass. Their fingers touched. A tingle arrowed through her, white-hot and trembling. Recalling how lost she'd felt at a single touch of those lips, she fought her growing ardor and forced herself to keep her eyes on his face. "Were you very humiliated?" she asked softly.

"After waiting till I was thirty-six to take the plunge? What do you think?" Dillon gave her a cocky grin that belied the hurt in his words. He set the glass on the bedside table and climbed beneath the covers once again.

Hayley felt a rush of feelings that surprised her. "I'll tell you what I think," she said, rolling toward him. She, too, propped her head on her raised hand. "I think she's a fool."

"I doubt she'd agree with you."

"Precisely why she's a fool," Hayley quipped.

They both laughed softly. Hayley lay just as she was beside him, savoring the darkness and the intimacy. It was a good feeling.

Dillon aimlessly caressed the blanket again. "Anyway, now you know why I want to keep up the charade while the kids are with us," he said. "If Marge ever got wind of this—"

Hayley tore her eyes from the caressing motions of his hand. "I see your point." He'd be doubly humiliated. "I'll do my best to play the role of the loving wife for the next twenty-four hours," she promised, wishing whimsically for a moment that her "duties" could include making love with him.

"Speaking of which, that dinner you fixed was delicious."

"Thanks."

The silence stretched out between them, even more comfortable now. Intimate. He gave her a sexy grin. "Now about this blanket," he began, palming the mound between them purposefully. All they had to do, she knew, was remove it and roll toward each other.

Hayley put her hand firmly on top of his, stilling the aggressive, male strokes. "It stays, Dillon." Satisfied she'd kept him from removing the only thing between them, she lifted her hand. "And it's a line you'd better not cross," she warned. Because Heaven knew what would happen if he did.

"Damn," Dillon said.

Her feelings exactly.

HAYLEY HEARD the alarm clock buzzing, as if from a great distance away. Too warm and comfortable to want to get up, she burrowed deeper into the covers, loving the coziness of the mattress beneath her and the hard male body cuddled next to hers. Thighs pressed against thighs, hips against hips, her back cossetted by the warmth of his chest. Even nicer was the strong arm wrapped around her waist. It curved just beneath her breasts.

Her head clearing, Hayley jerked awake. Dillon sat up, too. Their sleepy glances collided. He looked as stunned as she felt. "Don't blame me—" he put up a hand before she could speak, then pointed down "—I'm not the one who hopped the line!"

Hayley glanced down and was even more mortified. Dillon was right. She was the one who had come over to his side of the bed.

Reaching behind him, he slammed off the alarm clock.

"Sorry," Hayley mumbled, trying to get clear of him.

"Not so fast." He caught her arm, drew her down and positioned himself between her legs in one swift motion. "As long as we have a few moments, let's talk about what we're going to do today."

Hayley stared up into his beard-roughened face, aware her heart was beating double-time. Lower, there was a peculiar fluttery feeling in her middle. "Fine," she said, ignoring the telltale tingling in her breasts, the lassitude in her thighs and the hard implacable ridge of his own arousal. "But I don't think your bed is the place to do it."

Dillon grinned, the morning beard on his face making him look all the more dark, dangerous and alluring. He captured her hands with his and held them loosely on either side of her. "I think it's the perfect place."

"You would," Hayley retorted. It wasn't a compliment. She bucked in an attempt to get him off.

He bucked back and playfully tightened his grasp on her wrists. "Whoa. You're not getting away from me that quickly, not when you broke the rules."

Hayley's nipples had tightened into aching buds of arousal. "What rules?"

"About staying on your half."

"I was asleep, for pity's sake!" she exclaimed.

"Aha," Dillon exclaimed in a voice accented heavily with Viennese. He peered at her in an imitation of Dr. Ruth. "So it was a subconscious move toward me."

Telling herself it would be undignified of her to struggle further, Hayley lay perfectly still beneath his weight. "It certainly wasn't conscious!"

"Sure about that?" Dillon taunted playfully, wedging himself in even tighter between her thighs.

"Very." Though she meant her voice to sound commanding, it came out breathless. "Now let me go."

"After," he said softly, his voice so low and sexy she should have known.

"After what?" Hayley asked.

He didn't reply. He didn't have to. His mouth came down on hers, touched briefly, then moved to the nape of her neck, where it traced sensual patterns of his own design. "You smell good," he murmured. "Like perfume and you and warm sheets."

"Dillon…" The moan swept through her, as fiercely as the sensual waves. He let her hands go, and they came up to press against his chest. "Dillon, don't."

"Don't what?" he asked idly, as his mouth moved beneath her jaw, down her throat. His tongue dipped inside the stretched-out neck of the old sweatshirt to trace her collarbone.

Hayley's pulse jumped erratically. She knew she was perilously close to losing all. "Don't do that!" she gasped.

"Don't do what?" he asked innocently, laughter in his eyes. His mouth moved lazily to her ear. "Don't do this?" He caught the lobe between his teeth. "Or this?" He kissed her squarely on the mouth and pressed his arousal even more firmly against her.

She burned like fire. And it was a fire only he could put out. "Dillon, please," Hayley moaned. This wasn't fair and he knew it, damn him!

"I want you, Hayley," he whispered softly, looking deep into her eyes. The intensity of his dark blue gaze held her mesmerized. "I want you all the time," he confided as he tunneled his fingers lovingly through her hair. "I think about you night and day. At the office. On the train home." His gaze ardently traced the contours of her face, lingering on her every feature in turn. "It doesn't matter what story is breaking, you're all that's on my mind these days." And then he kissed her again. And again. Hayley surged up against him, loving the taste and touch and smell of him.

If it hadn't been for the footsteps moving down the hall, past his bedroom, Hayley knew what would have happened. But there were footsteps. Definite footsteps. And the knowledge of the other people in the house was all the impetus she needed to stop him once and for all.

"No, Dillon." She tore her mouth from his and pushed him away. "No."

At the seriousness in her tone, he drew back. She saw regret in his eyes and genuine disappointment. She knew it was over. For now.

"No go, huh?" he teased as she breathed a halting sigh of relief.

"Definitely not," Hayley said. She was furious. How could he be so composed when she had nearly come undone?

Hand to his chest, she pushed him firmly out of her way and, arms and legs flailing, fought her way out from beneath the covers.

She was in a standing position in the very center of the bed when he caught her ankle. "We still haven't discussed our plans," he reminded her patiently.

With his tousled hair, bare chest and silk pajama bottoms that hid nothing of the shape of his male anatomy, he was as tempting and therefore as dangerous to her as ever. Hayley looked down at him and folded her arms across her chest. "Okay, what are yours?" she asked contentiously. No matter what he did he was not getting her beneath him again!

"To get ready for the party," Dillon offered innocently.

Reminded of that, knowing the preparations for it were likely to keep them both very busy, Hayley relaxed a little. "Where are we having it again?" she asked.

"At the Hilton."

"So what do you have to do?"

"Nothing, really." Dillon shrugged. "The hotel's doing everything. I just thought you might have something you want to do."

Where he held it, Hayley's ankle was growing warmer.

"Some renovating project?" Dillon prodded.

Hayley swallowed. "Actually I was thinking about reinforcing that banister on the stairs. I have all the materials in the garage. I just need a block of time."

"Consider it yours," Dillon said generously.

Hayley sent him a narrow glance. "You'll watch Christine for me?"

"Cara and Vickie will. I'll help you with the banister."

Hayley grinned. Try as she might, she couldn't picture Dillon with tools of any kind. He was much more at home with a teletype, fax and computer. "Sure about that?"

Dillon shrugged. "How hard can it be?"


"YOU'RE DOING IT again," Dillon informed Hayley several hours later.

Hayley straightened slowly, trying hard not to let on just what that low sexy voice of his did to her. "What?" she asked drolly. Her insides had not turned to mush just hearing the sound of his voice!

Dillon gestured at her hair. "Trying to make yourself look like a housewife with all those green and pink spooly things in your hair."

"They're curlers," Hayley corrected dryly. "And they're in my hair so I'll be sure and look beautiful at your sister's party tonight."

Dillon sauntered closer. "Whether your hair is straight or curly or in curlers doesn't matter. You're still beautiful."

Looking into his eyes, Hayley could believe it.

Determined, however, not to let him get to her in the sensual way he had that morning, she volleyed back, "Are you here to flirt or work?"

His eyes glimmered. "Do I have a choice?"

"No."

"Then it's work, I guess."

Hayley gathered up her tools. "You've probably noticed the posts that support the handrail on this stairway are loose."

"Yeah, I've been losing sleep over it," Dillon said. He unfastened her tool belt and put it around his waist.

Ignoring his antics, Hayley picked up a small wooden wedge that she'd cut the previous afternoon in preparation for this job. "We're going to tighten the balusters by driving small hardwood wedges between the posts and the handrail."

"Okay, I got it. I'll do it," Dillon said, elbowing her aside.

"Don't you think I should show you, first?"

"What's to show?" He slid the wedge in before Hayley could say a word and began hammering away. He knew the moment he'd seen her expression that he'd done something wrong. "What?"

"You were supposed to put glue on the end of the wedge before you hammered it in."

Dillon sighed. "All right. I'll take it out."

"No, Dillon—"

Ignoring her advice, he bent down, and with the anvil edge of the hammer, began trying to work the wooden wedge out.

"Dillon—"

"I've got it—"

"Don't—"

He reeled backward, lost his balance and walloped himself in the face with the metal end of the hammer in quick succession.

"Don't what?" Dillon said, rubbing his cheekbone below his right eye.

"I was going to say don't put so much pressure on the wedge," Hayley said. She winced as she saw where he'd accidentally clobbered himself. Turning on her heel, she said, "I'll get some ice."

When she returned, Dillon was seated on the stairs. Hayley knelt down beside him and pressed the ice bag to his eye. "You're going to have a shiner."

He grinned at her. "You probably think I deserve it."

"For that kiss this morning? Probably, but no one should hit himself in the face with a hammer, Dillon."

He lifted the ice bag, gingerly touched his cheek, and winced in pain. "Agreed."

"Oh, Dillon," Hayley sighed.

"Oh, what?"

He was such a klutz! She bent and kissed his forehead. "Oh, nothing."

He caught her wrist with his free hand before she could move away. "I disagree," he said softly. "It is something."

Suddenly Hayley was having a hard time dragging oxygen into her lungs. "What's something?"

"That kiss." His eyes searched hers meaningfully. "It was the first time, you know."

Would he ever stop trying to find a new angle so he could put the moves on her? "You've kissed me before," she pointed out.

"Yeah, I know, but that was the first time you kissed me."

So it was, Hayley thought. She drew back slowly.

"Wait a minute. Don't tell me," Dillon said. "That was an accident, too?"

Leave it to Dillon to try to make something out of what had really been nothing. "You're the one who's having the accidents," she said.

She reached for the wedge he had dropped. Dillon started to get up. She held up a halting hand. "No. Stay where you are, please."

"I can still help—"

"I know, but I don't want a black eye to match yours."

"Cute."

"I thought so." Hayley put glue on the end of the wedge and positioned it. "Besides," she said, "all I really need to make this work go quickly is a little company." She began to hammer.

Dillon caught a glimpse of himself in the hall mirror. He shook his head, examining the bruise. "Of all the inopportune times," he swore as he examined the tender skin. "Now the neighbors will really have something to talk about."

"Poor Dillon. Unlike us girls, you can't even use makeup to cover it up."

"I should hope not." He gave her a shocked look.

"This is all my fault," she sighed, taking back her tool belt and fastening it about her waist. "I shouldn't have let you assist."

Dillon shifted the ice pack slightly on his bruised face. "No, I'm just clumsy when it comes to tools. I always have been."

Hayley paused between wedges. "It bothers you, doesn't it?"

"What?"

"That I'm adept at this and you're not?"

He shifted uncomfortably and couldn't quite meet her gaze. "Why do you say that?"

Hayley shrugged. "Because it bothers most men. They consider tools their domain. It drives them crazy."

Dillon thought about that for a while. He peered at her

argumentatively. "And you don't consider the kitchen your domain?"

Hayley thought of all the meals she hadn't cooked him since she had moved in. "Don't you wish I did," she said.

"I don't know," he teased. "I kind of like the way you look in a tool belt." He sighed enviously, his eyes lingering on her slender hips. "Much better than me."

A heat flowed through Hayley that had nothing to do with her chore.

"We're back!" Vickie walked in carrying Christine. Cara followed bringing the stroller and diaper bags. All three had rosy cheeks and happy faces.

"I take it your walk to the park was successful?" Hayley asked, glad for the interruption.

"It was great!" Vickie said. "Except I think Christine got sand everywhere!"

"Oh, yeah, and here's your mail," Cara said, handing it over. "What happened to you, Uncle Dillon?"

"It's a long story," he replied morosely.

"We're going to take Christine to the nursery and get her cleaned up, okay? And we promised she could have more juice."

Hayley smiled at the three girls, thinking how nice it was for Christine to be around people who so clearly adored her. "I'm sure she'll like that." She smiled as the trio moved off.

Dillon finished thumbing through their mail. "Here's your half," he said, handing it over. "You've got three replies from publishers, too."

Hayley sat down where she was and opened the envelopes one by one. Each letter said essentially the same thing.

"Bad news?" Dillon guessed.

Hayley held in her disappointment as best she could. "They're all sorry, but they don't need my services at the moment."

"I'm sorry, Hayley," Dillon said gently. "I know how great your paintings are."

"That doesn't mean much, does it?" Hayley replied. disheartened. "I can't even get anyone to take the time to look at them."

"Maybe if you'd let me help—"

"Dillon, no," Hayley said swiftly.

"I could make a few calls, set something up," he continued helpfully.

Hayley shook her head. "I do it myself or I don't do it at all."

"Why are you being so stubborn?"

Hayley reached up to adjust a curler that was coming loose. "Because I owe you too much as it is."

"Don't kid yourself, Hayley," he said gruffly, meeting her eyes. "You're more than pulling your own weight here."

Hayley dropped her gaze. She thumbed through the polite rejection letters on her lap. "I still have to do this on my own. Otherwise I'll never really know if I'm any good."

"Of course you're good," Dillon protested. "I just told you that."

"Thanks, Dillon." She looked up at him, knowing he meant well. "But let's face it. You're no art critic. And even if you were, it's not your opinion that counts. Not this time."

# Chapter Nine

"Fabulous party, Hayley, you really outdid yourself."

"Thanks, Carol," Hayley said, as she and Carol wedged a place for themselves in the crowded reception room at the Hilton, "but I can't take any credit for it. Dillon did all the work—everything from selecting the menu for the buffet to picking out Marge's birthday gift from us." And though Hayley had appreciated not having to deal with any of the details of the party, she felt oddly left out, too. As if she weren't nearly as much a part of the festivities as he was.

Hayley glanced over at Dillon. In baggy white trousers, a tropical shirt worn unbuttoned to mid-sternum and with several fragrant leis around his neck, he looked handsome and relaxed, despite the purpling bruise that went from cheekbone to brow on the right side of his face.

"What happened to his eye?" Carol asked.

Hayley helped herself to a wedge of fresh pineapple from her plate and tried not to think about how she had kissed him to make him feel better. "He tangled with a hammer and the banister and they won," she told Carol wryly.

"You're kidding." Carol eyed Dillon up and down, her glance traveling from the top of his windblown hair to the visible strength in his girded thighs. "With those hands and that powerful build, I would have thought he'd know everything about tools."

The tools of love maybe, Hayley thought. Feeling herself blush slightly at the thought, Hayley remarked casually, "He's more at home with a teletype."

Carol sighed and nibbled on roast pork. "I guess you're right," she laughed softly. "With those bedroom eyes of his, who needs to know how to use a hammer?"

Nellie came up to join them. "So what's up?"

"We were talking about how handsome Dillon is," Carol said.

"I know. Even with that shiner...it's too bad he's not handier around the house," Nellie lamented.

"You heard?" Hayley asked. She hadn't realized how much the other women envied her because she was married to Dillon. Now that she knew, she felt almost jealous. She wasn't the type to get possessive about a man!

"Everyone's heard," Nellie replied. Her voice dropped a confidential notch. "He's not taking the ribbing all that well, either. Honestly, Hayley, don't you know better than to outshine your man? They need to feel smarter than us, even if they aren't."

"Oh, can the subservient malarkey, Nellie," Carol chided. "It's the Nineties."

"Mark my words," Nellie disagreed. "Some things never change. Cut a man off at the knees, and he'll find a woman who won't."

"Won't what?" Dillon asked curiously, coming up to join them.

Hayley and the other two women flushed guiltily.

"If I didn't know better, I'd think you ladies were talking about me," Dillon teased.

"Actually, we were saying what a great job you did

planning the party," Carol said. "The band you hired is wonderful."

"Speaking of that band, I want my wife to dance with me." Dillon led Hayley out onto the dance floor. One hand around her waist, he tugged her newlywed-close and whispered playfully in her ear, "You looked like you need rescuing."

"Carol's nice. And Nellie means well," Hayley murmured, trying not to notice how good it felt to be in his arms again, or how proprietorially he had splayed his palm across the middle of her bare back.

"Nellie giving you a tough time?"

The full skirt of Hayley's floral print sundress swirled around her legs, as the two of them swayed together, cheek to cheek. "Just advice on how to handle my man."

He arched his brow as he deftly kept time to the old Rodgers and Hammerstein tune. "What'd she say?"

"In a nutshell?" Hayley took a deep breath, the lifting of her chest stirring the delicate flower leis around her own neck. "I'm supposed to treat you like lord of the manor."

Dillon grinned. He urged her closer with the flat of his hand. Their bodies fit together as snugly as a lock and a key. She could feel his arousal and recalled all too vividly what a demanding and yet ultimately giving lover he had been. "Lord of the manor," Dillon repeated. "I like that idea."

Hayley burned everywhere they touched. Her nipples were aching. Her thighs were liquid, weak. Hanging on to her self-control by a thread, she pushed away from the evidence of his virility. "Well, I don't."

Dillon grinned at her unrepentantly. "I didn't figure you would." But he still wanted her, Hayley thought, just as she wanted him. More all the time…

One song ended, another began. "Have you been happy, living with me, Dillon?" Hayley asked eventually, wondering if what Nellie had said earlier was true, if she had unwittingly emasculated Dillon by her competence with tools. He certainly didn't act like it, though.

"Sure, I've been happy." Dillon slid his palm suggestively across her bare back, eliciting even more tingles of awareness. He smiled at her wickedly. "I could be happier, though."

Hayley stumbled, and then recovering, drew herself up taut. "I'm serious."

He grinned devilishly. "So am I."

Heat started low in her body and welled up, through her chest, neck and into her face. "Besides that," Hayley said as the fluttering in her tummy slipped a little lower.

Dillon leaned closer, pressed a light kiss to her flushed cheek and whispered in her ear, "Besides that what else is there?"

Hayley created more distance between them. "Love, trust and affection." The words were out before she could stop herself.

Dillon's eyes connected with hers and held a breath-stealing moment. "We could have all that," he said.

"Even the love, Dillon?"

At the mention of love, Dillon's steps faltered. He stopped moving and stood with his arms locked around her. "I would care about you, Hayley," he said. "I already do."

Hayley resumed dancing. Dillon followed, then took back the lead. "I've disappointed you, haven't I?"

Trying not to think how much she liked the tantalizing scent of his after-shave, Hayley shrugged and avoided his eyes. "You're only being honest."

"Yeah." Dillon sighed regretfully. "But I'd probably get further if I were a bold-faced liar."

Hayley ignored the way his hands had tightened possessively on her once again. "Don't count on it," she said lightly. "I can spot a fraud a mile away."

Aware as was she that their neighbors and his sister were watching the two of them dance with more than mild interest, Dillon leaned forward and pressed another light kiss against her ear. "Oh, yeah? Can you spot a man who's desperately in lust with you?" he teased.

Hayley grinned even though it angered her that he clearly only wanted a physical relationship. "I don't think you have a serious bone in your body, Dillon Gallagher," she accused with a bantering smile meant to disguise the way she felt.

The song ended. Hayley started to step away. Dillon held firm. "Not so fast, Mrs. Gallagher," he said as his blue eyes darkened ardently. "I've hardly seen you all evening. I want at least one more dance."

"You've already had three," she reminded him unsteadily.

"I want four."

"One more dance, Dillon," she agreed, swallowing around the sudden tightness in her throat. "Then I've got to find Christine."

Dillon used the back of his palm to urge her closer. "She's still with Marge," he told her, smiling contentedly. "And stop worrying. She's having a better time than you are."

Hayley glanced up, wishing their steps didn't fit together quite so well, wishing she didn't know what an insatiable lover he was. "How do you know?"

Dillon smiled. "I just do."

They danced some more. Hayley tried not to notice how

he rested his chin against her forehead as they danced. If she didn't know better, she'd think he was desperately in love with her.

"Of course it hasn't been just this evening," Dillon continued amiably after a moment.

Hayley blinked and tore her eyes from the strong column of his neck. "What hasn't been just this evening?"

"That I've missed you," he confessed. He pulled her closer, so they were touching everywhere. "I've been missing you all week," he whispered, his warm breath sending a thrill down her spine. "Every time I come home you've been working on that darn house—"

"That darn house is the key to both our financial futures, Dillon," she reminded, a bit too brusquely.

"What about us?" He leaned back, so he could see her face. "Don't you want to see more of me?"

She did and she didn't. "What do you expect me to say to that, Dillon?" She was as frustrated by their situation as he was. And yet she knew, as did he, there were no easy solutions.

"That you'll let Marge take care of Christine on Wednesday and come into the city and have lunch with me."

The prospect of an intimate lunch with Dillon made Hayley's heart beat even harder. He was up to something; she could tell. "Why Wednesday?" she asked.

He shrugged and determinedly held her gaze. "Why not?"

*Because if I did I might be tempted to make love to you again,* Hayley thought. And there were more practical reasons, too, she realized, as she considered all she had yet to do. Dillon felt she still had all the time in the world to finish their house, but she knew she didn't. If and when she landed work as an illustrator, she knew she would have to drop everything and pursue her career.

"I'm sorry, Dillon. I can't." His face fell as she continued. "I've already arranged to have all the old carpet taken up and carted away that day."

"So reschedule."

"I can't. It'd put me too far behind on the renovations."

"Back to the house again," he said grimly.

"It's important," she insisted.

Dillon's lips tightened unhappily. "More important than me?"

"YOU'RE STILL ANGRY with me, aren't you?" Hayley said hours later when the two of them were alone.

Dillon walked into the living room,. "You're right. I am ticked off. I've asked very little of you—"

"On the contrary," Hayley disagreed. "You've asked and taken a hell of a lot."

He flushed guiltily. His blue eyes probed hers. "If you're referring to our lovemaking—" he began, jaw tightening.

"Among other things."

He strode toward her, closing the distance between them in three masterful strides. He jammed his hands on his waist and faced her cantankerously. "As much as you'd like to pretend otherwise," he pointed out tightly, "that was a mutual decision, Hayley."

She tore her eyes from the whorling tufts of dark silky hair, visible in the open vee of his Hawaiian shirt. "One I wouldn't have made," she declared hotly, "if I'd not been so tired and wrung out and emotionally vulnerable that night."

A muscle worked in his jaw. His eyes were hard and

accusing as he rubbed a palm across his chin. "Did it ever occur to you *I* might have been tired?"

"Were you?" Hayley shot back.

"No," Dillon said honestly and without apology. His eyes held hers. "I knew exactly what I wanted and I went after it."

And he was still going after it, Hayley thought, as the breath left her lungs in one sudden whoosh. She pivoted away from him, afraid if she stayed there one second longer she would give in to the desire that had been dogging her all evening. "You really are a jerk sometimes!" She wished he wouldn't be so blunt about wanting her. Because whenever he talked about taking her to bed again, she was unable to think about anything else.

"But an honest jerk," Dillon countered. He followed her and stood behind her, putting his arms around her. "Come on, Hayley. Come into the city and have lunch with me on Wednesday."

Hayley leaned into his solid male warmth for one moment. It would be so easy to give in to him, she thought. "Maybe the week after next," Hayley conceded finally.

Clamping his hands on her shoulders, he spun her around to face him. "I want you with me Wednesday," he said in a voice that brooked no denial.

Her curiosity roused, Hayley asked, "Why? What's so special about Wednesday?"

He shrugged, his expression becoming remote, mysterious and altogether too choirboy innocent to be believed. "I've got a three-hour gap in my schedule. We could have a long lunch at the Algonquin."

And then what? Hayley thought. Retire to one of the hotel rooms upstairs that he'd just happened to rent in advance and that just happened to have a bed in it? And then just happen to make love? And just happen to end up with a broken heart at their year's end?

"Dillon, I can't. I'm sorry. Not this week," she said.

He stared at her in mute frustration, then seemed to come to some decision. "Fine," he said, as if her refusal to meet with him were ultimately of no consequence. "Be that way. I'll just have to manage without you, won't I?"

Manage what? Hayley wondered. Why was he being so damn mysterious? "Dillon—"

But it was too late. He'd already gone into his den and slammed the door shut behind him.


"IT MUST BE A RELIEF to get all that awful carpet out of your house," Carol said early Wednesday morning. "What are you and Dillon going to do with the floors?"

"Refinish some of them, recarpet the others," Hayley replied. She put a stack of letters in the mailbox, and put up the red flag.

"Hayley," Nellie began.

"Nellie—" Carol warned, an unusually harsh edge to her voice.

"I've thought over what you said last night, but don't you see, Carol? I have to tell her!" Nellie protested. "Carol, Hayley has the right to know."

"I'll probably shoot myself for asking this," Hayley injected drolly, "but the right to know what?"

Nellie swallowed. All the color left her face. "The right to know your husband is cheating on you, Hayley. And he's going to do so again today!"

Hayley's heart seemed to stop. For a moment she couldn't even manage to draw a breath. "What are you talking about?" she asked finally, amazed at how normal her voice could sound when her pride was at stake.

"My Bob overheard him talking to Chuck, his brother-in-law—"

"I know who Chuck is, Nellie," Hayley rejoined sarcastically.

"Last night on the train home," Nellie continued, savoring the gossip. "He said he was furious with you for not meeting him in town for lunch today, but it no longer mattered. He knew what he had to do and he'd decided to take action anyway."

"Take action?" Hayley echoed. True, Dillon hadn't had much time for her since the party the previous Saturday. But she'd thought...he'd said he had an enormous workload at the office.

"He was going to meet this lady friend of his at the Algonquin Hotel—"

"Nellie," Carol injected firmly. "You've said quite enough."

"Hayley has a right to know!" Nellie cried.

"I think since you've already told me part of it, you'd better tell me the rest," Hayley said.

"He said since you wouldn't cooperate with him, he was going to have to look for 'solutions' himself." Nellie continued like a harbinger of doom.

"Solutions?" Hayley echoed weakly, feeling ill and betrayed.

"Hayley, I think he's starting to run around again, just like he did in his bachelor days. Marge said he could never seem to settle down with just one woman. Why, even when he was engaged before, he couldn't go through with it and called the whole thing off just days before the wedding."

Hayley leaned against the mailbox. "I know all about that."

"Did you know about his meeting with another woman at the Algonquin Hotel today?" Nellie persisted.

No, she hadn't. But Dillon had asked her to meet him there first.

"I'm sure it's something innocent," Carol protested.

"How innocent can it be if Hayley didn't know about it?" Nellie countered.

How innocent indeed? Hayley wondered. "Actually, I did know about it," Hayley admitted slowly. She warned herself not to jump to any conclusions. Despite Nellie's certainty, they didn't yet know what any of this meant. "He wanted *me* to meet him in town for lunch today," Hayley continued.

Carol put her arm around Hayley's shoulders. "I'm sure there's a good explanation for all of this, Hayley." She shot an irate look at her friend. "And I told Nellie that last night."

"I'm sure there is, too," Hayley said with a great deal more confidence than she felt.

"Well, don't just stand there. Stop it!" Nellie implored her urgently. "Stop Dillon before it's too late."

"If what you've told me is true, if he is meeting someone else there, it's a little late for that," Hayley said dejectedly. After all, she and Dillon had agreed they could look elsewhere for sex prior to their marriage, as long as they were discreet. And, in Dillon's defense, he had asked her first.

"It's never too late if you love someone," Carol put in sternly. "The question is do you love him, Hayley? Enough to fight for him?"

A SCANT HOUR LATER Hayley was on the train into the city. Still half out of breath from her mad dash into the house to change into something city slick and fantastic, she leaned back in her seat and looked out at the pastoral countryside whizzing by. Fortunately Nellie and Carol had agreed to oversee the removal of the carpet for her. Marge still had Christine. She had the rest of the day, indeed as much time as she needed, to square things with Dillon. But did she want to square things with Dillon?

Hayley shut her eyes. How had it come to this? Why was she rushing back into the city to chase after any man? After all, Dillon was only doing what they had agreed before their marriage that he could do. It shouldn't be any surprise to her that he was meeting his sexual needs with another woman. Dillon was a very physical, passionate man. He had asked her to make love with him again. She had turned him down flat. He had tried to woo and seduce her. She had turned him down flat. He asked her to lunch. She put him on hold. He had practically begged her to cancel her plans. She had still said no. She had given him no choice but to seek female companionship elsewhere.

Was she as desperately in love with Dillon as Carol thought? Hayley didn't know. Dillon made her laugh. He made her furious. He made her want to love again and be loved. But there, their compatibility ended. She wanted a pastoral life in the suburbs, a career that would enable her to stay home and be there for Christine while she was growing up. Dillon found the suburbs stifling. He could've cared less about the house. He hadn't promised that they could have anything more than a satisfactory business arrangement and a good time in bed.

So why was she chasing after him?

"MAY I HELP YOU, miss?" the maître d' asked.

"Dillon Gallagher," Hayley panted, still feeling slightly out of breath. She combed her fingers through her hair. "Is he here?"

"Yes, but his party is already here, miss. And they have requested complete privacy."

Hayley's heart sank.

"If you wish, I could—"

"Maybe we're not talking about the same Dillon Gallagher," she interrupted hopefully.

"Miss?"

"This is a big city," Hayley rushed on, telling herself there had to be some mistake. Dillon just wouldn't do this to her. She swallowed hard. "Probably there are a lot of Dillon Gallaghers," she said airily. She leaned closer to the maître d' and whispered conspiratorially. "So, you see, if I could just see him and he couldn't see me…"

"Miss." He looked grievously affronted. "This is highly irregular—"

Hayley slid a twenty into his palm. "I know it is, sir," she agreed, her eyes holding his in one last desperate hope. "Perhaps this will help ease the way."

He pocketed the money unobtrusively. "I suppose if you were to be seated at the bar and kept your back turned, you would not be seen. Mr. Gallagher seems to be quite interested in what his companion has to say, anyway."

He wasn't kidding, Hayley thought. Dillon was sitting so close to her in the booth he was practically in the young, good-looking redhead's lap, Hayley fumed. Their heads were bent together. They were laughing and talking. Just looking at them made her physically sick.

Having seen enough, she left without ordering, headed through the lobby and back out onto the street.

Dillon hadn't lost any time in replacing her, she thought numbly. All she'd ever been to him was a convenience. And that's all she would ever be.

"ARE YOU MAD at me?" Dillon asked hesitantly that night.

Hayley sent him a stony look and continued sanding the floor. "What would make you say that?"

"Well, for one thing, dinner was fixed when I got home."

"What's so shocking about that?" Hayley retorted sharply, noting he had changed out of his more formal work clothes and into a sweater and slacks. "You hired me to fix your dinner, didn't you?"

"Yes." Dillon looked confused. "But you never do."

"You're never home," Hayley shot back.

"I was tonight." He followed her around as she continued to sand the floor.

"So I see," she retorted. Unable to control her raging temper, she ran the sander a little closer to his feet.

He leapt out of the way in the nick of time to save his toes. He gave her a dark look. She gave him one. "Can you turn that thing off so we can talk?" he shouted.

She remembered how he had cozied up to the redhead just hours ago and gave him a cold look. *I have nothing to say to you,* she thought. But not about to add to the humiliation she had already suffered at his hands, she retorted with as much civility as she could muster. "I have work to do, Dillon."

"It'll just take a minute." When she continued to ignore him, he reached over and switched off the machine.

The silence was as deafening as the machine had been. She wished he didn't look so damn good, or that her insides weren't knotted up. She had actually cried all the way home on the train, oblivious to the stares of strangers. She felt worse than she had when Hank had been killed.

For so long she'd been focused on her dream. She'd thought all she needed for herself and her child was a nice home in the suburbs. Her relationship with Dillon had made her question that. Now she wasn't so sure a house in the suburbs was the answer. She'd almost rather have Dillon, even if he was never going to be committed.

She'd thought she'd had enough uncertainty in her youth to ever live the gypsy life-style again. Yet here she was, actually considering chucking all she'd worked so hard to garner just for the sake of being with Dillon! And that was crazy!

"Well, what do you want?" she asked him grumpily.

He studied her wordlessly. Finally he said, "There's a party to welcome me back to the States, being held in my honor Friday evening. It's at a co-worker's house, here in Connecticut. I'd like you to go with me."

Hayley was barely getting through the day. She knew she couldn't possibly play the loving wife for an audience again. Not after what she'd seen. "I don't think I can get a sitter," she lied stiffly.

"I'll talk to Marge."

She moved to turn on the switch. His hand shot out and clamped down over hers, preventing her from resuming her chore. "It's important to me, Hayley," Dillon said, his eyes holding hers. "And it's important to you," he finished gently.

Hayley had the feeling no party would ever carry as much weight with her as it did with him. But she also knew she owed him. Like it or not, she had to see this thing through. She had to finish the renovations of the house and sell it. She had to find another way to support herself and her child and find a decent place, hopefully in the tranquil beauty of the Connecticut suburbs, to live. Then she could take her money and run.

"Fine," she snapped, shoving a hand through her disheveled hair. "What time do I need to be ready to go?"

Dillon continued to study her like she was a subject in a medical survey for PMS. Finally he said, "I'll be home to get you around seven." He paused, still looking at her weirdly. "The people there will be pretty dressed up. Suits, ties, cocktail dresses, that sort of thing."

"I won't embarrass you with the way I'm dressed," Hayley promised. Jerking her hand from beneath his, she turned the floor sander back on.

But given her current mood, that was all she was promising.

# Chapter Ten

"You're fighting back, aren't you?" Carol crowed in the Saks Fifth Avenue dressing room Thursday morning. "I knew it."

Hayley examined herself from every direction in the three-way mirror, looking to spot the tiniest flaw in either the dress she had on or herself.

"What are you talking about?" she asked Carol, distractedly.

"That drop-dead cocktail dress you've got on, of course."

Hayley motioned vaguely and wondered if she needed some sexy new shoes, too. Maybe black silk stockings with seams in them. Men really seemed to go for those. Would Dillon? Not wanting Carol to know how desperate she felt to hold on to him, though, or how pitiful she felt her desperation was, Hayley dismissed her actions. "Don't make too much of this, Carol. I just needed something to wear to the party for Dillon tomorrow night."

"Something to wear or something to make his eyes bug out of his head?"

Hayley's glance collided with her friend's. "Okay," she admitted ruefully, blushing. "Maybe I do want to remind him of what he's given up, chasing skirts."

Carol grinned. "Locked him out of the bedroom, hmm?"

*He was never in.* "Let's just say certain marital privileges have been indefinitely suspended." Hayley turned, so Carol could help her get the dress off.

"Hayley, you dirty dog."

Hayley stepped out of the circle of incredibly soft and alluring black silk. "Dillon is the dirty dog."

"Agreed. Why'd you let him get away with it?" Carol asked.

"I haven't!" Hayley protested.

"But have you confronted him?"

"No."

"Why not?"

Hayley shrugged, feeling more lost and lonely than ever before. "Because it would be ugly and unproductive."

"I don't know about that."

"I do," Hayley said. "And I hate scenes like that."

"It might clear the air."

And it might end their marriage. "I don't have time for that." Hayley waved Carol's suggestion away. "Besides, I have a house to finish, remember?"

Carol replaced the first dress on the hanger and handed Hayley another. "And then?"

Her expression downcast, Hayley slipped into yet another drop-dead dress, this one in scarlet. "And then if the marriage isn't working, it isn't," Hayley said.

Carol frowned as she zipped Hayley up. "I still think you should talk to him."

"And say what?" Hayley asked. "That Nellie clued me in and I spied on him? He already thinks the suburbs are claustrophobic because everyone knows everyone else's business."

"This is a *bedroom* community," Carol teased.

"Very funny."

Carol's expression grew concerned. "Are you sure you're going to be all right, Hayley?" she asked.

"Why wouldn't I be?" Hayley discarded a tenth dress and reached for number eleven. Never had she had so much trouble finding something suitable to wear.

"It's not good to hold so much anger inside."

Hayley turned to face Carol. "You think I'm angry?"

Carol merely raised a brow. "You're telling me you're not?"

DILLON LET OUT a wolf whistle when he walked in the door at seven Friday evening. "Wow."

"That's what I said." Marge grinned.

"Looks like I've got a wife who really knows how to party," Dillon said. He offered her his arm. "Ready to go?"

Hayley nodded, her rage giving her strength. Before this night was over, she was going to have every man there eating out of her hand. And Dillon was going to know what it felt like to be on the outside, looking in.

The drive to Dillon's co-worker's home, where the party was being held, took a little over twenty minutes. Dillon made a few attempts at conversation, then fell as silent as she. "I'll be introducing you to my boss at NCN this evening," Dillon said as they started up the front walk of the gracious Colonial house.

"Is he married?" Hayley asked.

"No. Divorced." Dillon paused. "Why?"

"Involved with anyone?" Hayley persisted, ignoring his question.

"Not seriously." Dillon gave her another curious look. "Why?"

Hayley shrugged nonchalantly. "Just wondered, that's

all." She didn't want to cause trouble for another woman. She did want to get back at Dillon.

"There are some other people I want you to meet, too," Dillon continued, ringing the doorbell. "One of my buddies, Harry Mulvaney, and his wife, Patricia. This is their house."

The door swung open. They were ushered in by a tall, almost homely man with thinning ash-brown hair.

"Hey, Harry," Dillon said easily, smiling at their host. "How's it going?"

"Great! Almost everyone is here." Harry took Hayley's hand and shook it warmly. "Hayley. It's nice to meet you. Dillon talks about you all the time."

Hayley blinked as Dillon helped her off with her coat. "He does?"

Harry hung her coat in the front hall closet with the other coats. "Sure," he said. "For instance, I know you have a baby daughter who's every bit as pretty as you. That you're interested in art. You paint like an angel. And you know everything there is to know about home repairs. Which is good 'cause Dillon here couldn't fix the latch on a briefcase."

"You flatter me, Harry." Dillon looked past Harry at the crowd of people already in the living room. "Where's Patricia?"

"In the kitchen, I think, readying another plate of appetizers. Go on in. Introduce your good-looking wife around."

"Harry's right," Dillon said as they moved off. "You are beautiful. And that dress," he groaned softly, so only she could hear. "God, Hayley, that dress. The black silk clings to you like a second skin."

Having met her first objective at "Operation Giving

Dillon a Taste of His Own Medicine,'' Hayley merely smiled.

The next few minutes were filled with introductions. To Hayley's continued discomfort, Dillon's co-workers couldn't have been nicer, or gone more out of their way to make her feel at home. Hayley was beginning to have doubts about what she'd planned, thinking maybe this wasn't the time to make Dillon pay for his intimate lunch...until Harry's wife came through the swinging louvered doors from the kitchen.

Staring at the gorgeous red-haired woman, with the all-too-familiar face and fabulous body, Hayley nearly dropped her drink.

"What's the matter?" Dillon said.

"Nothing," Hayley mumbled. Except one big thing. Harry's wife, Patricia, was the woman Dillon had been with at the Algonquin. Did Harry know? More to the point, how could Dillon let Harry and Patricia throw a party for him when he and Patricia...dear heaven, she couldn't even say it to herself!

"Hey, Patricia!" Oblivious to Hayley's stunned and furious thoughts, Dillon waved. "Come on over here and meet Hayley."

Patricia handed the tray to Harry to pass around and threaded her way through the guests to Dillon's side. "Hayley. It's so nice to meet you," she said softly, in a warm, cultured voice. "Dillon's told me so much about you."

Hayley tried valiantly, but remembering all too well what she'd seen Wednesday afternoon, was unable to completely suppress her anger. "I'll bet."

Dillon's eyes widened. Patricia shot Dillon an uncertain look before turning back to Hayley once again. "Dillon tells me you're interested in a career as an illustrator,'' Patricia continued with grace.

"Yes, I am, but I'd rather talk about you," Hayley said. She gave the other woman a slick smile. "How long have you and Harry been married?"

It was Patricia's turn to look surprised. "Why. Almost a year, I guess."

"Happily?" Hayley prodded.

"Hayley!" Dillon reprimanded.

Patricia laughed. She touched Dillon's arm with a soft looking, impeccably manicured hand. "It's all right, Dillon. Yes, Harry and I are happy, Hayley. Deliriously so." She stared straight into Hayley's eyes.

If she had an ounce of guilt about what she was doing, Hayley thought, she wasn't showing it.

"Why?" Patricia continued.

Hayley shrugged. "I just wondered."

"Not that we don't have our problems." Patricia laughed softly. "We do. There are times, like tonight, when I'd like to kick Harry from here to China."

Dillon grinned and turned to Patricia intimately. "Why? What'd he do this time, Pat?"

"Forgot the ice. Would you believe he had to run out and get some, just ten minutes before the party was to start?"

Hayley slipped away while Dillon and Patricia were still deep in conversation about Harry's latest foible. She hadn't even gotten as far as the fireplace, where a fire was crackling, when she was joined by a dapper-looking man in a navy blazer and gray wool slacks. His dark blond hair was neatly combed. He had an aristocratic face and a smug courtly manner that screamed Ivy League.

His gaze raked her figure thoroughly. "Nice dress."

"Dillon likes it," Hayley said, distracted, as she went

back to thinking about "Operation Giving Dillon a Taste of His Own Medicine" and the advisability of implementing it now.

"I wager he does." The dapper stranger stuck out his hand. "I'm Chip Wilson, Dillon's boss at NCN. My family started the network years ago, and I took it over when my father retired."

"Hello, Chip," Hayley said. "It's nice to meet you." And now that she'd met him, Hayley wasn't so sure she wanted to put the moves on this guy, even if it was to pay Dillon back. He seemed nice, if not her type.

"I've got to tell you," Chip continued pleasantly. "Dillon's indispensable. I couldn't run the USA Bureau without him. Of course, no one thought Dillon would ever get married or come back to the States to work again, especially after that broken engagement."

*He hasn't,* Hayley thought, *not really. Not the way everyone thinks.* He was only back in the States temporarily, to please Marge. He was only married to save her reputation, and perhaps himself some trouble with his house.

Hayley took another sip of her wine. Across the room Dillon was still intimately engaged in conversation with Patricia. Seeing their heads bent together conspiratorially now reminded Hayley of the lunch. She burned with jealousy. Aware Chip was still waiting for some sort of comment from her about her new husband, Hayley tried like hell and failed just as mightily to keep the asperity out of her voice, "Oh, Dillon's full of surprises."

"Not all good?" Chip presumed quietly, a speculative light gleaming in his pale green eyes.

Out of her peripheral vision, Hayley saw Dillon chuckle softly. He bent and lightly kissed Patricia's brow. Just the way he sometimes kissed her. His hand moved across the smooth skin of her bare back. Just the way he sometimes touched her.

*Fine,* she thought. Two could play at this game. Two would.

Hayley fanned herself dramatically. Aware Dillon was watching her now, Hayley asked Chip, "Do you think it's hot in here?"

Chip warmed to the unexpectedly smoky note in her low tone. "Getting hotter all the time," he said flirtatiously with a grin.

Aware Dillon was frowning, Hayley slipped off her rhinestone-studded bolero jacket. The front of her black silk dress was slashed dramatically in a vee nearly to her waist. The back, from waist to nape, consisted merely of a weblike series of crisscrossing string ties.

"My dress feels a little loose." Hayley complained to Chip in exactly the same kind of voice she imagined Patricia had just been using on Dillon. "Tighten the strings—oh say half an inch or so—would you please?"

Chip hesitated only momentarily. "Sure," he said, as if it were the most natural thing in the world.

He quickly undid the bow, tugged the strings the requisite half inch and began to retie the bow. Dillon had noticed. He wasn't coming over. Yet. "A little tighter, Chip," Hayley said.

"Okay. Here goes." Chip had just grasped the bow a second time when a shadow loomed over them.

"Hello, Chip," Dillon said grimly. "I see you've met my *wife.*"

Chip looked at Hayley nervously. "Maybe we'd better let Dillon do this," Chip said, still holding the ties to her dress.

"Let Dillon do what?" Dillon asked grimly, glaring at Hayley.

Hayley returned his reproving look with a saccharine one of her own. Who did Dillon think he was, anyway? Coming over as if he *owned* her? He wanted all of the privileges but none of the responsibilities of a relationship or marriage.

"As you can see, Hayley's having a little trouble with her dress," Chip said.

Still seeing red over Dillon's possessive attitude, Hayley shrugged in a manner meant to irk Dillon even more. "Nothing Chip can't fix."

"True," Chip replied tactfully, letting Dillon know with a glance that if any hanky-panky had been going on, it wasn't of his making. "Perhaps Dillon should act as your valet, though," Chip said firmly. "She wanted it a little, um, tighter."

"Thanks for your thoughtfulness, Chip, in stepping aside. Don't mind if I do." Dillon gripped Hayley's dress by the strings and hauled her away, picking up her discarded jacket with his free hand. "Excuse us. We'll be right back."

"You're making a spectacle of us."

"No," he corrected as he steered her into a powder room at the end of a long hall. "*You're* making a spectacle of us.... Okay, what the hell's going on?" he demanded as he shut and locked the door behind them.

"I don't know what you mean," she said, now holding her dress strings.

"Then I'll enlighten you. First you're borderline rude to Patricia, then you're coming on to Chip, who's all but drooling over you to begin with! Not to mention the fact that he's my boss. I don't know what the devil has gotten into you the past few days," he lamented. "But you are acting crazy."

*Like he didn't know why!* "What'd you expect, bringing me here?"

"I don't know," Dillon countered sarcastically, looking more angry and hurt now than confused. "Maybe that you'd be as nice to my friends as they're trying to be to you."

"And you!" Hayley cut in curtly.

"What's that supposed to mean?" Dillon demanded. He backed her up against the vanity, so they were standing face-to-face, his hips pressing into hers.

"Like you don't know," she sneered, aware he was beginning to be as aroused as she.

"I don't!" Dillon complained.

"Patricia!"

"What about her?" Dillon asked impatiently.

Hayley felt herself go very white, then very red. "I know, Dillon."

Dillon blinked and stepped back. "Oh." He was quiet a long moment, looking every bit as guilty as Hayley had expected him to look when confronted with his betrayal. Her heart sank as she realized it was true. Dillon was carrying on with Patricia. He had all but admitted it now. Why then didn't that make her happy? Hadn't she wanted him to tell her the truth?

"How'd you find out?" Dillon asked.

"I don't see how that matters," Hayley said stiffly, turning away from him. She longed to splash some cold water on her face. Anything to make herself feel better. But doing that would ruin her makeup.

"It matters to me," Dillon said. He stood behind her, several inches away.

Looking into the mirror, Hayley caught his eyes. "I saw the two of you together," she said.

"When?" Dillon bit out, looking more aggravated than guilty now.

*There'd been more than once?* Hayley thought, astonished. She whirled to face him, her fingers itching to slap his ruggedly handsome face. "Wednesday, at lunch. When did you think?"

He shrugged negligently. "It could have been Thursday."

Hayley's jaw dropped. "You met her for lunch then, too?"

"Sure," Dillon shrugged. "Her and one of her friends."

It was Hayley's turn to blink. "There were three of you?" Hayley gasped.

"Well, yeah," Dillon said as if it were the most natural thing in the world for him to be dining intimately—and heaven only knew what else—with two women simultaneously. "Patricia doesn't edit children's books. Her friend does."

Children's books! Hayley stared at him. "What are you talking about?"

"You told me you knew," he said, exasperated, throwing up both hands. "Leah's an editor at Franklin and Lowe Publishing Company. So's Patricia. They're colleagues. I asked them on the sly to help me get you your first contract as an illustrator. What'd you think was going on?"

"Nothing," Hayley denied swiftly, her face flaming. Desperate to get out of the closed space, she tried to step by him. He put out a hand and wouldn't let her.

"You thought I was—" His eyes narrowed in sudden recognition. "Damn, Hayley, Harry's my friend!"

"Meaning what?" Hayley shot back sourly, irritated she'd been so far off the mark. "It'd be okay if he wasn't?'' Not giving him a chance to answer, she hop skipped on to her next complaint, one that was all too valid and true. ''Besides which,'' she continued grumpily, ''I told you I didn't want your help careerwise.''

''But it's okay for me to help you out personally, by marrying you, and economically, by offering you a job,'' he surmised sarcastically.

Again Hayley's face flamed. ''That's different!''

''I don't see how,'' he disagreed just as vehemently. His hands came up to cup her bare shoulders. ''It's okay to accept help from people, Hayley.''

No, it wasn't, Hayley thought. ''Oh, Dillon, you're so naive.''

''How am I naive?''

Hand to his chest, she shoved him aside. ''You think everything is so simple, when I know it's not. Friends are only friends as long as you're not a burden to them. Once you become a liability, then you're a noose around their neck. As far as the house goes, we both know I'm more than earning my keep and at the end of the fix-up process, we'll both realize huge financial gains. But the job—''

''I made two phone calls and sprung for two lunches. That's not so much,'' Dillon pointed out, advancing on her.

''But there's no way I can pay you back.'' He was so close, Hayley had to tilt her head back to see into his face.

He shrugged. ''You could give me a painting. For my new house.''

''Right. Of bunny rabbits and teddy bear characters?''

''I wouldn't care what it was,'' Dillon insisted stubbornly. ''As long as you did it.''

Silence. ''I care about you, Hayley. Of course, there's a part of me,'' he teased, ''that wants you to be green with jealousy whenever you see me with another woman. As jealous as you are tonight.''

Hayley tossed her hair. ''I am not jealous.''

They were so close they were touching. ''Yes, you are.'' His sexy grin widened. ''And that business with Chip just now. You were trying to make me jealous,'' he accused, fingering a thick wave of honey blond hair.

Irritated he saw so much of her true feelings, when she wanted him to see so little, Hayley swatted his hand away. ''I wanted you to know what it felt like to be humiliated, okay? Now can we go back to the party?''

He tilted his head to one side. ''I thought we needed to fix your dress.''

Hayley wished she could reach her bolero jacket and cover up a bit, but it was still hanging haphazardly on the towel rack next to the door where he had left it. She pretended to adjust the neckline a little higher and said stiffly, ''It's fine.''

''No,'' he drawled, disagreeing. His gaze drifted sensually over both her breasts and the imprint her raised nipples made upon the silk, then back to the center and the shadowy hollow between them. ''It looks a little loose to me. Yep,'' he said, as he reached behind her and swiftly took the strings of the criss-crossed ties from her. ''In fact,'' he said, undoing the strings all the way up the back. ''It's completely undone!''

The front of her dress fell free. Hayley's hands instinctively went to her chest, before the front could go any lower than the uppermost curves of her breasts. Blushing furiously she held the fabric to her and fought to maintain as much modesty and dignity as she could. ''Dillon, tie it back,'' she instructed sternly.

His humorous grin only widened. ''Why?'' he taunted. Finding it far too dangerous to face him when she was thus indisposed, Hayley pivoted and offered him her back. She heaved a beleaguered sigh, letting him know in no uncertain terms by the distinctly unamused gaze she tossed him over her shoulder that she was finished playing games. "Because it will fall off if you don't."

"So?" He grinned at her, teasing now as his palms ghosted playfully down her spine, up again and over her shoulder blades. "I like you half-naked, remember? I think I like you even better completely naked."

"Dillon," Hayley moaned desperately, shutting her eyes. She knew it was her own fault she was in this situation, but she wanted out, before either of them did anything they would enjoy but later regret. "Please—"

"I like it when you beg, too," he whispered, bringing his hands around her rib cage, and up. He touched her breasts, traced the heavy milky white weight.

"I've never begged."

"You will." He kissed her ear. She threw her head back. He kissed her upraised throat.

Knowing she'd be lost if he did much more of this, Hayley jerked her head away from him. "Save it for your other lady friends," she growled. She was hoping against hope she could start another argument and save herself from this fate.

No such luck. He wasn't taking offense. He wasn't taking anything but increasing pleasure from fondling her breasts and pressing up against her.

"Jealous, huh?" he whispered in her ear. "I kind of like that."

"I am not!" Hayley cried hotly, pulling away from the pleasurable torture of his hands.

"Are, too." His hands on her shoulders, Dillon turned her swiftly. His mouth covered hers. Giving her no chance to protest, he kissed her long and hard and deep. She moaned low in her throat and put a hand up, to push him away, but all she ended up doing was holding him even closer.

"Oh, Hayley, I've missed you," he groaned. His hands slid down her hips. He pulled her even tighter against him. She felt his arousal, pressing against her. His tongue stroked hers lazily as her middle fluttered weightlessly.

The next thing she knew, he had lowered the front of her dress to her waist. His hands cupped her breasts and nimbly worked the nipples to aching crowns. He kissed her again and again, so thoroughly that her knees went weak and she whimpered against him.

"Dillon, we can't—" Hayley pressed at his chest.

He released her slowly. "I know. But I want to." His eyes connected with hers and held. "And so do you."

He doesn't love me, Hayley reminded herself sternly. As ardent and fulfilling as his lovemaking is, it's all just a lark to him. A temporary solution to a very immediate problem. She'd always been more sensible than that.

"There are a lot of things I want, Dillon," she said as she turned around and readjusted her clothing with shaking hands. "I deny myself things because they're not good for me in the long run. Too much chocolate, for instance."

Dillon reached for the ties that had held the back of her dress and began lacing them through the loops. "Comparing me with candy. I like that, too. It's sweet." He tugged the ties tight. "If you're worried about calories, don't be. Making love burns them off, it doesn't add them on."

Hayley caught his glance in the mirror. "But it leaves me open to another kind of risk," she pointed out. "I don't particularly want my heart broken, Dillon."

He wrapped his arms around her and held her close. "I won't break it," he said.

"Maybe not intentionally," Hayley pointed out.

Dillon was silent, apparently having no immediate rebuttal for that.

Hayley shrugged out of his embrace. "People are going to wonder what we're doing here." She reached for her bolero jacket and put it on.

Dillon stopped her at the door. "This isn't finished, Hayley. Not by a long shot. But we'll put it on hold," he promised her huskily. "For now, but only because I can see you're not ready to take it further."

Hayley tried not to think how right his lips felt on hers. "I'm not sure I'll ever be ready for a love affair with you, Dillon," she said.

"Then I'll be disappointed." He kissed her brow lightly and hugged her close. "But I'm not giving up. We've got incredible chemistry, Hayley. And that doesn't happen every day. It'd be a crime to waste it."

"It'd be more of a crime to begin something wildly satisfying we know is only going to end."

"No, Hayley," Dillon said. He cupped her chin and brought her mouth to his. With the mood between them, she expected hot, sexy, fireworks but he gave her slow, gentle passion, moving his lips over and over hers until they parted helplessly under the onslaught, and she was meeting him touch for touch, stroke for stroke. Until she was moaning softly in her throat and clinging to him helplessly.

And it was then he broke the kiss, looked down at her and said, "It's more of a crime not to experience it at all."

"I'M SORRY I was rude to you earlier," Hayley told Patricia after all the other guests had left.

"Dillon explained to me about the mix-up. Your reaction was understandable."

"I shouldn't have jumped to conclusions."

"Let's just forget it and concentrate on your new career," Patricia said, pouring them each more coffee. "Your illustrations are exceptional, and I'm not just saying that because of Dillon. If they stunk, I'd say so." She smiled warmly. "They don't. Of course I don't work in the children's books department. My friend Leah does. She liked your paintings, too, and would like to meet with you. I have her phone number." Patricia wrote it down for Hayley "You can call her on Monday and set something up."

Hayley folded the paper and slipped it into her purse. She was embarrassed about the way she had behaved earlier, but thankfully Patricia didn't hold it against her. "Thanks."

"Good luck, Hayley. With the job and with Dillon."

Together they walked out to the living room to join the men. "You and Harry are very close to him, aren't you?" Hayley asked.

"We are." Patricia smiled. "And Dillon's a great guy. You're lucky to have him."

THE ONLY PROBLEM WAS, Hayley thought later as she wandered around their big empty house in her pajamas, that she didn't have Dillon. Not really. He had married her because it was the only way she would agree to stay. And that was hardly the precursor for future happiness or stability.

And yet, Hayley thought, as she sat down on the stairs and surveyed the progress she was making on the foyer and living room, he made her feel like no other man had. When he kissed her, she felt increasingly complete, increasingly impatient for more. She wanted to make love to him, to know what it felt like to wake up in his arms every day. She wanted a future with him, the kind he couldn't give. She couldn't seem to help wishing that would change, though, that one day soon he'd realize he loved her and would become committed.

A shadow fell across her. "Hayley?" Dillon whispered. He came down the stairs and sat beside her. Clad only in his pajama bottoms, his hair a rumpled sexy mess, he had never looked more handsome or more ruggedly appealing to her.

"What are you still doing up?"

"Too much coffee at the end of the party, I guess. I couldn't sleep."

"Me, neither. But my problem isn't the coffee," Dillon confessed, taking her hand in his. "It's the things I didn't say to you tonight."

Hayley's pulse speeded up as she anticipated the worst.

"You know how I accused you of being jealous of Patricia?" he asked.

Hayley nodded, her mouth dry.

"Well, I was jealous, too, when I saw you with Chip. To the point I didn't care if I made fools of us both. I never felt that way before."

"Join the club." Hayley leaned back against the step, so her shoulder was touching his. "I've never acted so foolishly, either." Recalling, Hayley moaned. She buried her face in her palm. "I can't believe I actually came on to him."

"I couldn't believe it, either," Dillon recollected grimly, then teased, "I wanted to punch his face."

"Why?" Hayley bantered back lightly, taking comfort in the fact they could always talk like this, no matter what else was going on. "He wasn't doing anything."

"Yeah, well, he wasn't resisting very hard, either," Dillon groused.

"He turned tail soon enough after you walked up to join us."

"True." They both laughed softly, recalling the stricken expression on Chip's face when he'd confronted Dillon's jealous wrath.

"What a night," Dillon lamented.

"And then some," Hayley agreed.

They were silent. Dillon's hand tightened on hers. He took a deep breath. "I realized something else tonight," he confessed.

"What?" Hayley asked hoarsely.

His eyes searched hers. "I don't want you to leave," he said softly. "In fact, I don't think I want to sell this house at all, even after it's finished."

Panic swiftly set in. Hayley sat up quickly. "But you said—"

"I know." Dillon held up a palm to stop her protests. "I didn't think I could fit in here, but it's grown on me. I like coming home to you and Christine every night. I like having a family, even if we're not really a couple."

"What are you saying, Dillon?"

Dillon hesitated only briefly. "That we should stop avoiding intimacy with each other, give our relationship more of a try."

"You're talking about making love again," Hayley ascertained, disappointed.

"More than that," he said quietly, studying her reaction gravely. "About being a couple. You know. Parents to Christine. All of that."

Her heart pounding, Hayley lifted her eyes to his. "And man and wife?"

Dillon shrugged. ''Or some facsimile thereof,'' he said casually.

Hayley let out her breath slowly. She wanted to give it a try, more than Dillon could ever know. She also realized they had to be practical about this. The house was months from being finished. She could imagine how hellacious it would be to live there if she and Dillon tried to be a couple, couldn't and hence weren't getting along anymore. ''If we did that, if it didn't work out, it could ruin everything,'' she said slowly, her heart pounding with the extent of her potential loss.

Dillon smiled, looking happier and more optimistic than any man in his situation had the right to look. ''Yeah, but if it does work out, we could have everything, Hayley. At least think about it,'' he urged.

She promised she would.

## Chapter Eleven

"Mama!" A plaintive voice echoed in Hayley's ear. She opened one eye, to see Dillon standing next to her bed, Christine cradled in one arm and what looked like an aluminum cookie sheet covered with a tea towel in his other hand.

"Wake up, sleepyhead," Dillon said as he bent and gently let Christine down on the bed. "It's time for breakfast."

"I never eat breakfast in bed," Hayley protested sleepily as Christine bounced cheerfully up and down.

Dillon reached behind Hayley and propped her pillows up against the headboard, so she could sit up. "Then it's time you started, don't you think?" He fit the aluminum cookie sheet over her lap. "I made enough for all of us."

"So I see," Hayley said, staring down in amazement at the awkwardly arranged dishes before her.

"If you have a real tray down there, we couldn't find it so Christine and I improvised," Dillon continued conversationally.

Hayley grinned, both amused and pleased. "I noticed," she said wryly. "And it was a good choice."

"I thought so. Anyway, we've got everything we need." Dillon caught Christine as she hopped by, and settled her comfortably on his lap. "Toast, jam, juice, and—" He held up Christine's Mickey Mouse thermos victoriously. "Fresh hot coffee for you, miss."

Hayley stifled a yawn. "How long have the two of you been up?" she asked.

Dillon shrugged. "Couple of hours, I guess. We wanted to let you sleep late."

"Thank you. I haven't done that in...maybe a year?" she guessed.

"See," Dillon nudged Christine, who was contentedly munching on a triangle of golden toast, "I told you she needed to be spoiled a bit."

Christine giggled at Dillon's teasing tone.

Dillon looked back at Hayley. "So what's on the agenda today?" he asked.

"I was going to run errands. Go to the supermarket and the bank, pick up the drycleaning, take Christine to story hour at the library."

"Want company?"

Hayley's heart skipped a beat. "Dillon—"

"What?"

She flushed at the intensity of his gaze. "It's a little boring for you, don't you think?"

His eyes held hers. "I'm never bored when I'm with you."

Hayley released a wavering breath. She'd thought Dillon had been pursuing her avidly before. She was beginning to see she hadn't experienced anything near his "full court press."

"Besides, I'd like to do all that family stuff with you and Christine," Dillon continued.

"You'll tell me if it starts to get to you?"

"I've never been shy about bailing out before."

"So how'd I do?" Dillon asked several hours later as he and Hayley sat with their feet up on the coffee table in his study. An exhausted Christine slept in the portable crib nearby.

"You mean except for almost getting us kicked out of the library for arguing with the puppeteer during story hour?"

"I couldn't help it," Dillon protested. "She was telling that story all wrong. The prince is never rescued by the princess. The princess is always rescued by the prince."

"Chauvinist," Hayley teased.

"Dreamer is more like it." He wrapped an arm about her shoulders and coaxed her into the warm curve of his body. "Although I gotta admit I wouldn't mind being rescued by you."

*I wouldn't mind rescuing you,* Hayley thought.

"Hayley?"

"Hmm?"

"Given any more thought to that question I asked you last night?" he asked softly.

"About us giving our relationship more of a try?"

He lifted one of her hands to his lips and caressed it softly. "That's the one."

"Dillon!" Hayley protested. Her merry laughter filled the room. "It's only been a couple of hours!"

"Long enough for you to make up your mind?" he asked hopefully.

He was more than meeting her halfway, Hayley knew. The question was, could he keep it up long-term?

If he did, she knew without a doubt what her answer would be. Yes, to everything he wanted from her.

The problem was it would take time for her to know for sure whether or not Dillon would eventually feel stifled and burdened by a wife and child.

"Dillon, I can't commit myself to anything just yet," Hayley replied softly. As good as she felt, wrapped in the warm curve of his arm... "I need more time."

He searched her face, then smiled slowly. "But you're leaning my way, aren't you? You're weakening," he crowed triumphantly.

Hayley couldn't deny it.

"YOU LOOK HAPPY," Marge said the following Wednesday. "The job interview must have gone well."

Hayley took off her coat and set her portfolio and handbag aside. "It did," she admitted as she kicked off her high heels. "Leah said she'd call to tell me definitely one way or another later this afternoon."

"I wish you luck."

"Thanks. But I can't take any of the credit. I owe Dillon for this one. He's the one who set up the interview."

"It's unlike him to get involved that way. Oh, he's been a mentor to many a cub reporter—"

"Like Hank—" Hayley interjected.

"Right. But never outside his own field before."

Hayley smiled, thinking how well everything had been going. She'd thought Dillon would've lost interest in her and Christine by now, and especially in all things domestic, but he hadn't. Oh, he would never be keen on washing dishes or doing laundry, probably never be any good at it, either, but he was trying, and he genuinely cared about her and her baby.

"The house is taking shape, too." Marge glanced around admiringly.

"I know. Dillon's even been pitching in to help. Believe it or not, Sunday he helped me operate the paint sprayer so we could refinish the kitchen cabinets. And we did it without a major catastrophe."

"No more black eyes, hmm?"

"Not so far. And last night? He helped me repair some grouting."

Marge raised her arms to the heavens in evangelical exultation. "Will miracles never cease."

They both laughed softly at her antics.

Shyly, Hayley said, "Could I ask you a favor? Would you take Christine for me for the night?" On the train back she'd come to an important realization and made some decisions. She knew now time would not change what she and Dillon had, except perhaps to make it stronger. Knowing that, it was time she paid Dillon back for all he'd done. It was time she met him halfway.

FOR A MINUTE Dillon thought he'd walked into the wrong house. There was furniture in the living room, a fire in the grate and a table set for two in front of it. Hayley lounged on one of the sofas in an emerald green silk shirt and black suede skirt he'd never seen. She looked more beautiful than he'd ever seen her.

He tore his eyes from the opaque black stockings and black suede shoes. Too late...the blood was already rushing to his lower half. "What are we celebrating?" Dillon worked to keep his voice casual. It wasn't easy, considering the heat and tension stiffening his groin.

Hayley smiled at him, raised her champagne glass in silent toast and said softly, "I got the contract, Dillon. Thanks to you and Leah, I'm going to be illustrating my first children's book. If all goes well, and I expect it will, Leah said I can count on many more contracts from their company."

"That's great." Or was it? Dillon wondered, panicked. Did it now mean she was one step closer to leaving him?

He watched her bend forward from the waist to pour

him some champagne. She'd left the first three buttons undone and he saw a hint of cleavage and what appeared to be a black lace bustier that was sexy as hell in the open vee of her blouse.

"Where's Christine?" he asked, annoyed at the sudden hoarseness in his voice.

Hayley lifted the necklace around her neck, then let it fall again, to nestle in the shadowy hollow between her breasts. She answered playfully. "She's at Marge's, spending the night."

As his eyes held hers, he noticed her irises were unnaturally bright, as if she were up to something deliciously naughty. "If I didn't know better, I'd say the scene was set for seduction," he teased, as he accepted the drink she gave him.

Hayley uncrossed her legs and bounced lithely to her feet. The next thing he knew her arms were laced around his neck. His nostrils were filled with the rich floral scent of her perfume. "Who said it wasn't?" She guided her mouth to his.

Their lips touched. Another bolt of fire missiled into his groin. Dillon groaned. Resisting Hayley under normal circumstances was damn near impossible. He was no saint. "Hayley—" he warned, not really sure she knew the full consequences of what she was doing.

"Dillon—" Hayley mimicked his cautionary tone, then quickly unknotted his tie and slid her hand inside his shirt to caress his chest. "I want you."

Had this happened any other time. Any other day. But knowing she had just today gotten a job, because of him, made the words Dillon had longed to hear for weeks now fall flat. "Why, Hayley?" he replied, his heart racing as the blood pumped into his groin. "Why now?" As much as he desired her, he had never wanted a "duty toss in the hay" from her. And knowing how Hayley felt about not being indebted to anyone, for anything, that had to be *exactly* what this was.

"Why?" Hayley echoed. She shook her head at him in amusement. "Because you've made such a difference in my life," she said, as if her coming on to him *now* were the most natural thing in the world, the most expected thing.

Alarm sounded in his brain. His chest constricted, making it hard for him to breathe. Dillon caught her caressing fingers in his hand, forced them to be still. "What do you mean?" he asked tersely. *I hope to God I'm wrong about this.*

Hayley stood on tiptoe. She left a string of kisses on his jaw. "Why, the job, of course. Because of your persistence in helping me out, even when I didn't want it, I now have a start in a brand new career."

"In other words, payback," Dillon muttered grimly as his worst fears came true. Disappointment scored his soul.

"What?" Hayley blinked uncomprehendingly, the excited color draining from her face.

Still rigid with desire, he pushed her away. "You heard me, Hayley. I can't do this. Not now. Not like this. I *won't.*"

"Dillon—" Hayley gasped. She recoiled from him, as if his rejection were the last thing in the world she expected.

"I'm sorry, Hayley." He couldn't bear the feeling he was breaking her heart. He stalked past her roughly. "I need some air."

Dillon vaulted from the house without looking back. He felt like a heel, but he knew it would only get worse if he stayed.

Hayley fed the dinner she'd so lovingly prepared to the

disposal. She blew out the candles, put her silver and china away. She was just trying to decide what to do with the champagne when Dillon charged back in. Their eyes met. The air between them fairly crackled with electricity. She clutched the nearly full bottle in her hand and just barely resisted the urge to hurl it at his stubborn head.

"I'm sorry," he began grimly, shoving both hands through the wind-tossed layers of his dark hair. His handsome face was ruddy from the cold night air. "I shouldn't have walked out on you like that."

How right he was about that! Hayley thought. "You should be sorry," Hayley retorted. She'd put not only her pride but her *heart* on the line for him. And what had he done? He'd thrown her efforts right back in her face. He'd acted as if making love to her were a fate worse than death. Well, not again!

Hayley set the champagne down on the counter with a thud. She elbowed her way past him.

Dillon caught her by the back of the skirt and hauled her around to face him.

His face hardened. "Don't you understand, Hayley? I couldn't make love to you, not that way."

She took exception to his flat, pragmatic tone. "What way?" she bit out. Reaching around behind her, she tried to extricate his hand from her waistband.

"Out of gratitude," he said, tugging her nearer.

"Gratitude!" Hayley shouted, astonished. She flung her hair out of her face with a haughty toss of her head. "You think I'd do all this out of gratitude?" As if she were that dumb or subservient!

He stared down at her in gritty silence.

"Be honest, Dillon," Hayley snarled back. She stood before him, hands knotted into fists at her sides. "You walked out on me for only one reason," she asserted, her breasts heaving with every angry breath she dragged in. "To pay me back."

"Pay you back?" Dillon echoed, dumbfounded.

Hayley placed both her hands on his chest and shoved until he reeled backward. "For turning you down so many times."

Dillon tightened his grip on her and hauled her against him. "You think I don't want you?" he demanded hoarsely.

"I don't know what to think!" Hayley volleyed back, ignoring the way the hard ridge of his arousal pressed against her stomach and made her tremble. She broke away from him. Her black suede heels clattered on the kitchen floor. "And I don't want to discuss it!"

Dillon cut her off at the door. "No, Hayley," he said. His broad shoulders completely filled the exit, blocking her only escape. "You're not running. We're going to finish this discussion."

Hayley's temper flared and combined with her hurt pride. "I say we're not!" she shouted back. She attempted to stomp on his foot. He stepped adroitly aside. The grip on her shoulders tightened. Dillon stared down at her fiercely. She saw his frustration.

Abruptly his hold on her gentled. "If you didn't do all that out of gratitude, because I helped you get a job, then why?" Dillon demanded, his low voice underscored with both confusion and passion.

"Why do you think? Because I love you!" Hayley jerked free of him. "Though God knows why!"

"You love me?" Dillon echoed, stunned. He stared at her as if he couldn't believe what he was seeing and hearing.

"Yes," Hayley said furiously. "For all the good it'll do me!"

Dillon grinned as if he had just won the million dollar lottery. "Looks like I jumped to the wrong conclusion," he drawled.

Hayley didn't know why he had walked out on her. Nor did she care. She only knew that he had. And she wasn't going to forgive him. "You sure did," she retorted hotly, her temper flaring to new heights. "And now you can go bungee jump off the nearest bridge for all I care!"

Dillon laughed heartily. She turned around and took a swing at him. He ducked the blow, then came back at her before she could swing again. Anchoring one arm firmly beneath her knees, the other beneath her waist, he swung her up into his arms.

"Put me down, you big lug," Hayley said.

"Not until we start the evening all over again." Ignoring the way her legs kicked and her arms flailed, he carried her unperturbably over to the refrigerator. He opened the door with the toe of his shoe, then stared, perplexed, at the empty shelves. "Where's our dinner?"

Having concluded that all her struggles were for naught, Hayley settled down enough to give him a withering look. "You're looking in the wrong place, loverboy." She pointed to the garbage disposal. "I fed it to a more appreciative recipient."

Dillon threw back his head and laughed again, the melodious sound of his voice filling the room. Eyes twinkling, he drawled, "Darn. Guess we'll just have to go straight to the good part then."

"The hell we will! Put me down," she ordered crossly.

"Gladly, in due time," Dillon said.

"I mean now!" Hayley ordered.

"I know what you mean," Dillon concurred genially. Pivoting, he carried her out of the kitchen as if she weighed no more than a sack of feathers.

"Then why aren't you doing it?"

"Because you don't always know what's good for you."

Hayley gave him a you-can't-be-serious look and guessed sarcastically, "And I suppose you do?"

"Just for the record," Dillon drawled as he carried her into the living room, collapsed onto the sofa and pulled her across his lap. "I didn't walk out on you earlier to hurt you, Hayley. You have to know that's the last thing I ever wanted," he said huskily, his eyes roving her upturned face. "I was trying to save us both from making another mistake and doing something you'd later regret and resent me for. So I walked out. It was only later it hit me," he explained logically.

Her attention caught by the gentleness of his touch, Hayley prodded crossly, "Okay, I'll bite. This time. What hit you?"

"That our making love could never be a mistake," he said softly. He took a deep ragged breath. "I also came to the conclusion that we belong together. You can call it fate or happenstance or any damn thing you like, Hayley, but I want to be with you so much I ache," he finished hoarsely. "So I came back. And the minute I saw you standing in the kitchen, looking every inch as miserable and unhappy as I felt, I knew I'd done the right thing. We belong together, Hayley."

She was flooded with relief. Buoyant with joy. Happier and more hopeful about the future than she had ever imagined she could be. "Oh, Dillon, I thought all the good in my life was over," Hayley murmured.

"No, Hayley," Dillon corrected gently, taking her fully into his arms once again. He held her close. "There's still so much left. This is just the beginning," he promised. "For both of us."

"I THINK you're tipsy," Dillon noted gravely two hours later.

For someone who'd spent the past few weeks trying every ruse imaginable to get her back into his bed, he sure was taking his time about it now, Hayley thought. He'd insisted they order some dinner to make up for the one she'd tossed down the drain. Then they had to spend even more time listening to soft music, watching the fire and draining every last drop of the golden champagne. But thoroughly relaxed and filled with a warm mellow glow that seemed to get stronger and more passionate with every moment that passed, Hayley could hardly fault him for his chivalrous lack of haste.

However, she did take exception to his powers of perception. "I am not tipsy," she protested as Dillon put out the last remaining lights on the first floor and returned to her side.

"Then prove it."

Hayley let out a beleaguered sigh.

"Stand with your eyes closed. Right here in front of the sofa." Hands on her shoulders, Dillon placed her just so. "Now tilt your head up. And then back. That's it."

Hayley felt his breath flutter warmly over her closed eyelids, her nose, then her mouth. This wasn't like any sobriety test she'd ever witnessed on television.

"Feeling dizzy?" Dillon asked.

Deciding enough was enough, Hayley blindly anchored both arms around his neck. She opened her eyes. "No, but I want to be," she teased playfully. "Does that count?"

"I don't think so," he said gravely, shaking his head.

"Then, kiss me," she urged softly, "and I promise I will be."

Dillon's laugh was cut short by their kiss. Breaths mingled. Tongues touched. And suddenly neither one of them could get enough. He was kissing her like there was no tomorrow. For Hayley, today had never been sweeter.

She knew now what she hadn't before, that the two of them did belong together. Not just until the house was finished, his time in New York over, but forever. In a matter of a few short weeks, he'd become everything that mattered to her. She trusted him completely. She trusted him with her heart. "Dillon, let's go to bed," she whispered urgently, knowing at last that it was truly safe for her to depend on him.

He raised his head and grinned mischievously. "Let's not." His hands skimmed up her sides, over her ribs. He gently cupped the weight of both her breasts with both palms. His eyes met hers. They looked even darker, sexier, in the flickering firelight. "Let's stay right here and give our new living room a proper christening."

Hayley's heart skipped a beat. She smiled at him slowly, aware she had never felt sexier or more voluptuous in her life. "I like the way you think." *And I like the womanly way you make me feel.*

"Then we're even, 'cause I like the way you dress." He unbuttoned her blouse, parted the edges and tugged the hem from the waistband of her skirt. His gaze dropped to the soft curves spilling voluptuously over the lacy edges of her black lace bustier. Dillon sucked in a breath as his glance skimmed the rosy nipples visible beneath the transparent black lace.

"Still like the way I dress?" Hayley drawled.

"Even more." He rubbed his thumbs over the tender crests. "You are so beautiful, Hayley," he murmured hoarsely. "Dressed or half-dressed or any way at all." His eyes held hers with the promise of limitless nights to come. "Well worth waiting for."

Hayley's breath came in quick, shallow spurts. She reached behind her and drew the zipper down. "If you like that, wait'll you see the rest," she promised, as she stepped out of her skirt.

His rapacious gaze drifted lower, to the lacy black garter belt and opaque black stockings. Hayley'd been afraid when she bought them they were too much. Not "her" somehow. Now, watching his reaction, they seemed exactly right.

He hooked his hands in the triangular scrap of black lace. One palm touched the nest of golden curls. The other flattened against the small of her spine. Cossetted between the warmth of his hands, she arched against him. He stroked her dewy softness, moving up, in. She surrendered helplessly. "Oh, Dillon, I want you," Hayley whispered urgently.

"We have all night," Dillon reminded her hoarsely. He deepened his intimate caress, until Hayley's legs trembled and her knees went weak. Aware she could no longer stand even *with* his help, he smiled with thoroughly male satisfaction and collapsed onto the sofa, tossed off her panties, and pulled her across his lap.

"I intend to take all night," he continued, between deep passionate kisses. "We're going to do this right, Hayley. Slowly. Lingeringly. So there are no regrets. No places that go untouched. By the time tonight is over, I'm going to know every inch of your body. And you're going to know every inch of mine."

While his hands lovingly explored her breasts, Hayley took off his tie. She unbuttoned his shirt, helped him out of it and flung it aside. His pants followed. Then his shirt. Dillon never stopped touching her. She never stopped touching him.

Soon they were kissing again. Hotly. Rapaciously. Until

she no longer knew where her own mouth ended and his began. Impatient for more, even if he was willing to wait past the five-alarm fire stage, Hayley sat in his lap, so she was facing him, then knelt, her knees astride his thighs. Slowly she lowered herself. She took the hot, hard length of him and drew him inside, then drew herself up, so she was once again on her knees.

The gliding sensation of wet hot silk was more than he could bear. Dillon moaned and caught her hips, forced her down. "Hayley," he murmured. "Oh, sweetheart—"

"Every inch of me, Dillon," she whispered tantalizingly, the pleasure on her face mirroring his. "You said you wanted every inch."

She moved up. Gliding rapaciously over the rigid length of him like a too-tight sheath of hot, damp silk. He groaned again as she slipped free. Replaced her body with the softness of her lips, the light butterfly tease of her tongue. He'd driven her to madness. Now she drove him to the brink.

Hands on her waist, he urged her up and over him.

"Now?" Hayley whispered softly, linking her arms around his neck.

"Now," Dillon said, as her breasts brushed his chest. He plunged inside her, commanding everything she had to give, while at the same time availing every part of him to her. Their mouths met in a long soul-searching kiss while their bodies touched everywhere it was possible to touch.

And they moved together. Damn, how they moved. For the first time in his life, Dillon learned what it was like to be with a woman, heart and soul. Loving her with every fiber of his being. He hadn't known he could need a woman like that. But he did, he thought, as the inevitable climax came. God help him, he did.

## Chapter Twelve

"And I thought the honeymoon was over," Marge remarked as she came in the door, carrying Christine and a diaper bag brimming with clothes, bottles and assorted baby paraphernalia. She looked over at Hayley, who was busy compiling a special breakfast for Dillon. "You're positively glowing this morning."

"Don't sound so surprised," Hayley teased back. "Your brother is—"

"Yes?"

Hayley let out a contented sigh. "The sexiest, kindest, gentlest man I've ever known."

Marge's brow quirked. "I'm glad you think so," she said.

Hayley bit her lip. "I'm ashamed to admit I haven't always. Lately, well...I got really angry with Dillon when I found out he'd been going behind my back, trying to take care of me."

"Dillon told you what he'd done?" Marge looked amazed.

"Yes, but not until I'd already found out about it on my own. I have to admit I was pretty steamed. But finally he helped me understand he was only trying to help me out,'' Hayley said. And because he had, Hayley thought, she now had a start in a brand new career.

Briefly, Marge looked troubled. ''So you forgive him for not being totally honest from the first?'' Marge asked.

''Yes, although it wasn't easy for me to accept his help,'' Hayley admitted honestly. ''I'm a very independent person.''

''I know.'' Turning her back to Hayley, Marge took off Christine's jacket and hat and settled her into the high chair.

Hayley handed Marge a fresh, hot cup of coffee. ''You had doubts about me and Dillon from the very beginning, didn't you?'' she asked. ''Why?''

Marge shrugged, looking unwilling to get into it. Hayley waited. Finally Marge said, ''Because of Hank, I guess.''

Hayley stopped buttering the toast and stared at her, confused. ''Hank?''

''The way Dillon felt after his death,'' Marge explained. She handed Christine a small triangle of toast that Hayley had already prepared.

''We all mourned him,'' Hayley said slowly, aware this was one thing she and Dillon had never talked about.

''Yes, but as you now know, Dillon felt particularly bad about it because he was the one who recruited Hank to go to the Middle East and cover Desert Storm.''

Marge's words were matter-of-fact, yet Hayley felt as if an eighteen wheeler had slammed into her chest. The breath left her lungs. She sagged against the countertop and had to dig her hands into the ceramic tile to keep from collapsing altogether. Dillon had recruited Hank personally? No, it couldn't be, she thought numbly. But even as she denied it on one level, another part of her recalled

Hank talking about how great everyone at NCN was over there, in particular his bureau chief....

Marge rambled on, too lost in her own troubled recollections to notice how devastating this news was to Hayley. "Dillon felt terrible about it for a long time, even though there was no reason he should have felt guilty. I mean Hank knew the risks when he accepted the job over there. They all did. It was Dillon's job to make those assignments. He had no idea the army barracks was going to be hit. But I guess the two of you have worked all that out now."

*We're about to,* Hayley thought grimly. Tears stung her eyes. How could Dillon have deceived her and played her for a fool? Thankfully it seemed only she knew the depth of his duplicity. Everyone else assumed she'd been aware of what had happened. How little they knew! she thought bitterly. In reality he had lied to her from day one and was still lying to her.

Hanging on to her composure by a thread, Hayley drew another bolstering breath. "Would you mind taking Christine out for breakfast? Dillon and I could use—" Hayley was so furious she almost choked on the words "—some more time alone."

Marge grinned and shook her head at Hayley. "You two really are honeymooning," she teased, as Hayley felt the wall she'd built around her heart resurrect itself with alarming speed. She'd thought she could trust Dillon with her life. Apparently not.

"Sure, I'll take her until...say ten or eleven? Will that give you two enough time?" Marge asked.

Hayley thought about what she had to say to Dillon and knew it wouldn't take any time at all. "Plenty."

DILLON EMERGED from the shower to see Hayley leaning against the vanity, her arms crossed. She was still in her negligee, but she was no longer the happy contented woman who'd left his bed. Her face had a grim look that even their night of incredible lovemaking couldn't erase.

"Why didn't you tell me?" she asked flatly.

Dillon's heart slammed against his ribs as he wrapped one towel around his waist and used another to dry his shoulders and back. There was no missing the boiling fury and resentment in her jade green eyes. "Tell you what?"

"That you were personally responsible for Hank's death."

Her words were rapier quick and cut just as deeply. Like lightning, the guilt that had weighed on Dillon for months came back to him. He felt he couldn't breathe. Like he'd never be the same again. It had been hell, losing one of the reporters. Losing someone so well loved and young had been even harder.

Aware nothing would be gained from either of them becoming hysterical, however, Dillon brushed past Hayley and headed for his dresser. He casually pulled on his shorts and then a pair of slacks. The situation was bad, he reassured himself firmly, but not unsalvageable. And it wouldn't be unless he lost his head. "How did you find out?" he asked quietly as he pulled on a sweater.

"It doesn't matter," Hayley replied. She sat on the bed.

"I guess it doesn't," he said slowly. He sat down beside her and covered her hand with his own. "What is important is how we feel about each other."

Hayley jerked her hand from his. She leapt to her feet and glared at him. "And how is that, Dillon?" Anger glittered brightly in her eyes.

Dillon pushed slowly to his feet, his actions as deliberate as hers had been impulsive. "I thought after last night that would be obvious," he remarked calmly.

Hayley sent him a withering glance. "All that's obvious is the fact you deliberately deceived me, Dillon."

Had he? Dillon wished he could say he hadn't, but he knew that wasn't so. He had avoided telling Hayley of his guilt, because he hadn't wanted to deal with her pain. Dealing with his own guilt and sorrow had been difficult enough.

"All along you were just doing this for me because you felt guilty! All along I've been some sort of albatross around your neck." She slammed her fist down onto the marble vanity. The thud sounded in the silence of the room. She whirled to face him, the chiffon of her negligee swirling around her slender body like a tantalizing mist. "I suppose the fact I was the kind of albatross you could take to bed with you was some consolation," she said bitterly. "But not much!"

"You're overreacting," Dillon said grimly. Throwing everything away for something that could never be changed, no matter how they wanted to do so, was crazy.

"Am I?" Hayley shot back bitterly. "Can you honestly stand there and say you would have actually married me to save my reputation if you hadn't felt guilty as sin?"

"I married you because I didn't want you to leave!"

"You married me because you were sick with guilt!"

"That's not true! Okay," he relented, when she won their staring match, "maybe guilt was the reason I came to see you in the first place."

"Definitely—"

"And offered to do anything I could to help. But the rest of it, my giving you a job, my taking you to bed, even my marrying you and wanting this thing to work was because I loved you, Hayley."

"If that's so, why didn't you ever tell me that before?"

He stared at her in frustration. "I have."

"You've never actually told me you loved me."

"Words alone are empty promises as far as I'm concerned. I *showed* you how I felt in hundreds of ways."

"You mean you atoned for your guilt!" she corrected icily. "Dammit, Dillon." She picked up a tissue box and threw it at him. "How could you do this to me?"

Dillon caught the box. He set it aside and advanced on her slowly, deliberately. He took her rigid body in his arms. "What have I done except love you?"

"You mean make love to me," she corrected.

"What's the difference?" Cupping a hand on the nape of her neck, he tried to make her look at him. But she wouldn't, and she wasn't listening, either.

Hayley shoved herself away from him. "Yes, it's hunky dory now." She went on lecturing him, as if he hadn't spoken to her at all. "Because we're compatible in bed. But what happens when that changes, Dillon?" She whirled on him, her eyes glittering furiously. "What happens when the passion fades, when you lose interest in me the way you've lost interest in every other woman who's ever been in your life, including your fiancée."

"I explained that," Dillon interrupted archly, his own temper beginning to flare uncontrollably, too.

"Then you're going to want out," Hayley continued.

"If I want out," Dillon interrupted curtly, his expression serious, "it'd be because you're as stubborn as a mule. But I don't."

Hayley shrugged negligently, clearly not believing a word he had just said. "So you say now."

Dillon's jaw set. "You don't believe anything I've just said, do you?" he ground out.

Her chin lifted. She speared him with a censuring, holier-than-thou gaze. "I believe you mean well." She brushed past him deliberately. "Unfortunately that's no basis for a marriage. Nor is hidden guilt!"

Dillon stamped down the hall after her and followed her into her bedroom. "What are you doing?"

Hayley hurled a suitcase out of the closet and followed it with an armload of clothes. "I'm packing!"

"Again?" he drawled. Crossing his arms, he assumed a no-nonsense stance. "Haven't we been through this before?"

"That was *before* we were married."

He stepped in front of her and blocked her way to the dresser. "It was stupid and immature then. It's stupid and immature now."

Hayley circled around him and headed for the closet again. "No, Dillon, you're the immature one, to ever think this could work." She tossed out another armload of clothes, then another. "Dammit, you should have told me how you felt about Hank's death the first day we met."

Dillon ducked as a boot went whizzing past his ear. "I tried. But you told me you'd had enough 'tea and sympathy and all that went with it' to last you a lifetime. Remember?"

At that, her face grew pale, her shoulders stiffer. Hayley faced him. She looked more hurt than ever, but no less ready to forgive him. "Yes, I was tired of the condolence calls, of being hit on by the NCN guys like I was in dire need of a mercy session in bed," she said logically. Then, apparently unable to resist hitting him where it hurt, she said, "You know, kind of like the one you gave me *last night?* But I *never* asked you to lie to me—"

"Maybe not, but you didn't look a gift horse in the mouth, either, did you?" Dillon advanced on her, not stopping until they were nose-to-nose. He grasped her arms and held her in front of him. "You were only too quick to accept the job and the profits from the house, and later, even my marriage proposal.''

Hayley stood as still and unresponsive as a statue in his arms. "Only because you backed me into it by trashing my reputation with the neighbors first," she volleyed back curtly.

"I apologized for that!" Dillon said, releasing her. More frustrated than he could ever recall being in his life, he drove his fingers through his hair and struggled to regain control. "Look, maybe you're right," he said more reasonably at last. "Maybe I should've told you about my part in Hank's death before we were married, but—"

"But what?"

"But I was afraid it would upset you, and frankly I didn't see how it would help."

Hayley regarded him with mounting impatience. "Well, this in-depth discussion of your treachery isn't helping, either." She pushed past him and yanked open her dresser drawer. Grabbing a fistful of frilly lingerie, she stuffed it on top of the rumpled clothes already in her suitcase. "You feel noble now, Dillon. But I can tell you from bitter experience that sense of nobility won't last. Just like the relatives who took me in after my parents' death, soon you'll be wondering what you're getting out of this. Then I'll be a cross you have to bear."

"A pain in the butt is more like it." She didn't laugh at his joke. With a growing sense of helplessness, Dillon watched her stuff two filmy nightgowns on top of the tangled mess.

She swallowed hard and turned to him. "Don't you see?" she asked in a choked voice. "I can't bear to be a burden to you, Dillon."

"You won't be," he said, wishing he could make her believe that.

She shook her head. "Oh, Dillon, I already am a burden. You're just too proud to admit to yourself you've made a giant mistake. Fortunately for both of us," she finished stiffly, "it's one that can be swiftly rectified."

Hayley closed her suitcase. Clothes hung out over the edges on both sides. It refused to latch. She opened it again, tucked everything in and closed it again. This time, to Dillon's dismay, it did latch.

"I'll finish the house in the daytime, while you're at work," she announced in a cold, calm voice Dillon found much more terrifying than her anger. She took another deep, halting breath. "There's no need for us to see each other."

Dillon jerked the damnable suitcase from her hands and sent it flying across the floor. Her clothes spilled out. "You can have the damn house!" he shouted back. "It's all you ever cared about, anyway. Working on it night and day, to the exclusion of all else, even your new career and me!"

Hayley whitened and reeled backward, as if he had slapped her. "How can you say that to me?" she cried.

"Because it's true," Dillon said. "If you weren't ripping out the tile or resanding the floors, you were repairing the balustrade and tearing down drapes."

Thanks to her, everything tacky had been removed. The walls and floors were bare, ready for new covering. Everything in disrepair had been fixed or replaced. The entire interior had the "clean canvas" look of a brand-new house. And when she was finished, as she would be soon, their home would be the pride of the entire neighborhood! "This house looks a lot better because of all I've done!"

"Maybe so, sweetheart, but you moved in with one foot out the door, married me the same way, and even made love to me last night, thinking about how soon you could sell the house, take your share of the money and walk out! And there's nothing noble or selfless about any of that!''

"That's not true," Hayley interrupted heatedly, bright spots of color appearing in her cheeks. "Last night I wasn't thinking about anything but last night." *And how wonderful it had felt to be in his arms again.*

"Of course. I should have known," Dillon said grimly. "You never do think about more than the present, do you? That and your precious independence! All along, you were just waiting for the excuse that would enable you to cut and run. Now that you've found it," he finished sourly, "you can't wait to get out of here."

Hayley couldn't dispute the truth of that; she couldn't forgive him for the way he had misled her. She stared at him angrily. "You're being deliberately cruel," she accused.

"No, Hayley, I'm being honest," Dillon corrected. "And it's time you were, too. Face it, sweetheart. You're the one at fault here, the one afraid to take any risks. You're afraid if you start to need or depend on me, I'll start to need or depend on you. That would require some caring and commitment on *your* part, wouldn't it? Neither of which you are able to give."

He stared at her, his fury and helplessness mounting. "And now you're just using this as an excuse, aren't you? Because you want out. Not because of what I didn't tell you, but because of what I mean to you."

She stalked over to retrieve her suitcase. She picked it up and held it in front of her, at knee level, like a shield. "The only thing you mean to me is pain," she shot back.

"Oh, really?" He advanced on her slowly, his dark blue eyes holding hers. "Then why are you so afraid?" he taunted softly.

She tried to brush past him. "I am not going to listen to any more of this."

He grasped her shoulders and swung her around. "Oh yes you are. You're not dumping me and walking out on our marriage until I've had my say."

"Why? There's no point! You're wrong about me. You're wrong about everything!" It was Dillon's fault she was so hurt and disillusioned! Before he came into her life, she hadn't dared dream she could ever have it all. She'd contented herself with having a child to love and the hopes of finding a nice place to live. That had been it. Then he'd come along and made her want more. Which she had. Only to find herself cruelly robbed of her happiness once again.

"I wish I was wrong about it," Dillon said sadly. "But I'm not, am I, Hayley? You're afraid to love me, because to love me might mean one day you'd lose me, and then what would you do? How could you cope?"

If right now was any indication, Hayley thought, as she struggled with all her might to hold back her tears, not very well.

Dillon continued, looking more grim and unhappy than she'd ever seen him. "You'd rather spend your whole life alone than take the chance on getting hurt again, wouldn't you, Hayley?"

He was acting as if she were the one who had betrayed him, instead of the other way around! Before she could stop herself, Hayley cried, "If the misery and heartache I'm feeling now is any indication, the answer to your question is yes, I would rather be alone!" Because he was right. That way of life was safer!

He threw up his hands and pushed away from her. "Fine, then. Enjoy the safe place you've built for yourself, Hayley. Because that lonely little cocoon is all you'll ever have!''

"THE WHITE plantation shutters you've installed on all the windows are simply beautiful, Hayley," Marge said admiringly as Hayley took her on a tour of the downstairs. "I like them so much better than the ugly drapes that used to be on the windows. In fact, the whole house is absolutely gorgeous. I can't believe how quickly you finished." She admired the blue and white ceramic tile and coordinating wallpaper in the kitchen. The cabinets had been stained a pristine white. Balloon drapes in a country print let plenty of sunshine in through the bay windows in the breakfast bay.

Marge turned to Hayley gently. "What does Dillon think?"

"He hasn't seen it," Hayley replied numbly. And for Hayley, that had taken all the joy out of it for her.

"I'm sorry. I thought—" Marge hedged as they walked through the formal dining room, past the downstairs hall and into Dillon's den. Except for a thick layer of dust on all his home office equipment, it was exactly as he'd left it. "It's been several weeks now—"

"Three weeks, two days and four hours," Hayley supplied dryly, exiting the den as quickly as she had entered it. "But who's counting?"

Marge studied her as they walked into the formal living room and sat down in front of the fire roaring in the grate. "You really love him, don't you?"

Tears spilled from Hayley's lashes. "I wish I didn't," she whispered.

"Does he know?" Marge asked gently. She leaned forward to pour them both some blackberry tea from the silver service on the coffee table.

"What good would it do to tell him after the way I've acted? He told me he loved me and I kicked him out because I didn't believe him. Didn't want to believe him," she corrected.

"So? I know he still cares about you."

Hayley wished she could believe that. "Then why did he move out? Why hasn't he called or come by again? You know Dillon, Marge. When he sees something he wants he goes right after it. He doesn't let anything stop him." She drew a shaky breath, recalling how intense his initial pursuit of her had been, how mordantly quiet her life had been since the night he'd walked out on her.

Hayley'd picked up the phone innumerable times. She'd even taken the train all the way into New York one day. But in the end she'd known she couldn't pressure him that way. Whether Dillon knew it or not, he was noble to the core. She didn't want him taking her back out of guilt over what had happened to Hank. She didn't want to be a burden to him. He had to want her for her alone, flaws and all. Not out of any misguided sense of duty or obligation. Obviously now that he'd had the time away from her that he needed to think clearly, he had decided against further involvement with her.

"No, I have to face the facts. My overwhelming need for independence, my obsession with this house, destroyed whatever it was he felt for me. His continued absence is sending a clear message. He wants to move on with his life again. And after all that's happened," she said, "I really can't blame him."

Marge shrugged. "So what if you made some mistakes? What if you both did? It doesn't have to be the end of the road for you two. Regardless of what you said to each other, regardless of how he's acted the past couple of weeks, I know he still cares about you, Hayley."

Hayley knew that, too, deep down. Unfortunately, it was a lot more complicated than that. "Just caring about another person isn't enough, Marge," Hayley said. She traced the edge of her teacup. "Not to sustain a marriage that lasts a lifetime, and that's the only kind of marriage I want. One that's based on a love strong enough to endure anything."

Marge was silent a long time, as was Hayley. "What are you going to do now?" she asked finally.

Hayley shrugged dispiritedly. She had gone into this relationship with one foot out the door. But all that had changed because of him. She had never dared dream she could have it all. She had focused so much on her dream, but Dillon had stormed through the citadel around her heart and showed her she could have even more than a child or a house of her own. Now…now she knew material possessions weren't everything, weren't really even that important to her. What counted was having someone who loved you. Someone to love. Someone to tell your hopes and fears to in the quiet of the night. He wasn't just a potential husband or father to her child. He was the other half of her soul, the person who'd given her dream meaning.

She wanted all they'd shared back. But it was too late. He wasn't coming back to her. Not ever. Hard as it was for her, she had to accept that and go on. "I don't know what I'll do, Marge." Hayley shrugged. "I'll put the house up for sale, I guess, as soon as I can get Dillon to sign the papers." The house seemed so empty to her without Dillon. She knew she couldn't bear to live here much longer. The memories were so overwhelming. Just thinking about the way they'd made love here, the dreams they'd had, the laughter they'd shared, made her heart break a little more.

"Have you talked to him about it?"

"No." Hayley sighed. "And I'm dreading it."

"You should," Marge muttered.

Hayley glanced up, sensing a warning there. "Why?" she asked.

"Because both of you are acting like monkey's behinds." Marge set her tea down so abruptly it spilled over the rim of the cup and onto the saucer beneath it. "He loves you, Hayley, and I know you love him. That couldn't be clearer. Why the two of you can't just apologize for past mistakes, admit that to each other and get on with it," Marge declared in exasperation, "is beyond me."

"THERE'S AN OPENING for bureau chief in South America," Chip said. "I know your assignment here in New York was supposed to last indefinitely, and still could if it's what you want, but you could also take the job in South America."

Dillon sat back in his chair and propped his feet up on his desk. "Trying to get rid of me?"

"Trying to find a way to get you to stop pacing the NCN floors before you wear them out. You've been restless. Distracted. And if you don't mind my saying so, not exactly a pleasure to be around."

Dillon took another sip of the lukewarm coffee on his desk. It was as bitter as his mood. He glanced at Chip's concerned face, taking no offense since none was meant. "It shows, huh?"

"Along with the fact that you're not sleeping much. Or eating," Chip said, concerned.

Dillon put his coffee back on his desk. He put his feet on the floor with an irritated thud. "You're beginning to sound like my sister," he complained.

"Yeah, well, if she were here, she'd tell you to get a life and stop hanging around here eighteen, twenty hours a day. You ought to go home more, Dillon."

I had a life, Dillon thought, with Hayley. And it was a damn good one before it got blown to smithereens by his own dishonesty. "Can't," Dillon said shortly, in response to Chip's advice to spend more time in Connecticut.

"Why the hell not?"

Because he was currently sleeping at his sister's there and her meddlesome badgering was worse than Chip's. "I'll take the position in South America under advisement. When do you need an answer?"

"Couple days." Chip frowned. "Would Hayley want to live there?"

"Doubtful."

"Meaning?" Chip prodded.

*I don't want to leave,* Dillon thought. All he wanted was Hayley and Christine. But he'd blown that.

His mood grim, Dillon went to the window and stared down at the city lights. New York City had never seemed less appealing. Once, he'd gotten off on constant movement and constant change. Now all he wanted was the pastoral serenity of a certain white Colonial house in the Connecticut suburbs, the simple pleasure of going home every night on the train to his wife and kid.

"I never thought I'd see the day," Chip crowed, mistaking the reason behind Dillon's recent moodiness. "Dillon Gallagher. Among the ranks of the newly henpecked. She really did it to you, didn't she, buddy? Made you into some—"

Dillon cast a warning look over his shoulder. "Want to keep all your teeth, Chip?"

"You wouldn't hit me," he said with smug satisfaction. "Hayley would disapprove."

*Yeah,* Dillon thought, *she would. She'd consider it uncouth.* Another difference between them. "The satisfaction I'd get would be worth it," he told Chip, and he was only half kidding. These days he had the constant urge to punch something, anything. His frustration and unhappiness were that great.

"How is Hayley, anyway?" Chip asked. "She can't be happy with the hours you've been keeping here."

*I haven't a clue how she is,* Dillon thought. "Fine, I guess," he replied in a distracted, disinterested tone.

"You guess?" Chip echoed.

Dillon sent him a warning look. "Keep your paws off her."

"Why would I go after a married woman?" Chip retorted, confused. "Unless—" He snapped his fingers. "Say, the two of you aren't having trouble already, are you?"

*Trouble?* Dillon thought. Was that what it was called when the woman who had once adored him now hated his guts? The only thing he was sure about these days was that he missed Hayley more than he'd thought it possible to ever miss another human being. Christine, too.

"What'd you do?" Chip asked. "Fool around on her? No. Hayley's too pretty."

"Keep your compliments to yourself," Dillon growled.

"Jealous, too," Chip observed with a smirk. "This gets better all the time," he crowed, delighted. "So, how long ago did she kick you out? Let's see, it had to be about the time you stopped being fit for human company. Two, maybe three weeks?"

"Three weeks, four days, eight hours and twenty-one minutes ago. And she didn't kick me out," Dillon corrected. "I packed a bag and left."

Chip shook his head ruefully at Dillon. "You might be

a genius when it comes to sorting out the news and deciding who should cover what story, but you really are stupid when it comes to women, pal.''

"Thanks ever so much, Chip."

"If I had a woman like that—"

"Well, forget it, 'cause you don't.''

"I wouldn't leave her. Ever. And I wouldn't let her leave me. No matter how mad she got at me, no matter what we fought about, I'd find a way to work it out. Preferably in a New York minute. So, smart guy, how come you couldn't do the same?''

DILLON STEPPED into the foyer of the house. "I've brought the papers.''

Hayley moved toward him, her heels making a staccato sound on the newly polished wood floors. "Great." She bent her head to study them. He saw her hands tremble slightly. He also noticed she wasn't meeting his eyes.

"They're already signed.'' His voice sounded flat and emotionless, even to him. But inside, Dillon was shaking. So much was at stake this evening.

Hayley's head lifted. Dillon stared into her jade eyes with the gold-tipped lashes and thought but couldn't be sure he saw a sheen of telltale moisture there, despite the laudable coolness of her voice.

"Come on in, Dillon. Take off your coat. We still have a few things to go over.''

"Yeah, like what?'' he asked gruffly, although he was already humoring her by taking off his coat and slinging it over the banister. And he welcomed the chance to stay a while, for any reason.

"Like did you approve of the realty company I selected?'' Hayley asked huskily as she turned to face him. She swallowed, still studying him, gauging his reaction.

Her tongue darted out to moisten her softly glossed lips. "Your sister says they're the best."

Dillon shrugged. He could care less about who sold the place. "Sure, why not?" he replied carelessly as Hayley turned and led him into the bar she had set up in one corner of the formal living room. "They sold it once, didn't they? To me."

*And what a schmuck I've been,* Dillon thought as Hayley fixed them both a salutary drink. He came there expecting her to forgive him and take him in, to put all arguments aside and take him in her arms.

Instead, Hayley looked like she'd never felt or been better. Her hair was a glorious honey blond mane, falling in thick soft waves around her shoulders. She had on a chic white cashmere dress. The bodice snugly hugged her upper body and the slim skirt outlined her hips in alluring detail. His gaze drifting lower, Dillon noted she wore three-inch heels that made her legs look fantastic. With a great deal of effort, he managed to stifle a soft groan. He had never wanted her more in his life.

Hayley moved closer, in a drift of perfume. Her hand brushed his as she handed him a glass of champagne. Dillon took it, although he'd never felt less like celebrating. She took his other hand in hers. "Have a seat, Dillon." She led him to one of the overstuffed armchairs she'd had reupholstered in brocade.

He sat where she'd directed. Loath to let go of her, he used his grip to pull her down into his lap.

Rather than resist him, she grinned. "Getting to you, hmm?"

His eyes narrowed. "What?" he asked brusquely.

"Me."

Again it was all Dillon could do not to groan. He closed his eyes. "You always have."

"And always will, I hope."

The soft entreaty in her voice caused his heart to slam to a stop. Dillon paused. He opened his eyes and took a good look at her. This time he was sure there were tears in Hayley's eyes.

"I'm sorry, Dillon." Her green eyes shimmered with regret. "So sorry. I got you over here on false pretenses."

Dillon felt like he'd been sucker punched in the gut. Now what was she trying to tell him?

"I don't want to sell the house," Hayley confessed almost shyly as she played with his collar and the Windsor knot of his tie. "I never did. I—I just wanted to see you again, and I couldn't figure out any other way to get you here, so I sent you those papers and asked you to bring them by tonight."

Dillon started to feel better than he had in weeks. "The dress—" he began hoarsely, wanting to believe she loved him yet almost afraid to hope because of what he'd done and the way they had parted. "Your hair—"

"Is all for you," Hayley confirmed. Her sexy grin widened a little more. "See, I'm taking a tip from a guy I know. He once told me when he sees something he wants, he goes right after it, and he doesn't let anyone cramp his style. So—" She looked deep into his eyes. "That's what I'm doing tonight. I love you, Dillon," she said. "I love you with all my heart. I have for a very long time and I know now that I always will. I just thought you should know."

He stared at her, stunned, aware he'd never been happier in his life, as all the hopes and dreams he'd once had for them, and thought were dead, surged to new life. "Oh, God, Hayley. I love you, too." He grabbed her and hugged her hard. "I know I should have told you everything—about the past, about how I felt—but I didn't.

Mainly 'cause I was afraid I'd scare you away." He forced himself to go on. "Later, I was scared I'd lose you."

"That's never going to happen," she reassured him.

Contented moments passed as they simply held each other. It felt so good, Dillon thought, to have her in his arms again. He never wanted to let her go. And yet he knew there was still much they had to clear up before they really could go on. "Hayley?" His gut twisted into a knot of apprehension. "I'm sorry about what I said, about the house."

"Don't be." Hayley interrupted him and drew back to look into his face. "You were right, you know. When you said I entered this relationship with one foot out the door. I did. Maybe not intentionally, but I did all the same. I realize that now. I was just so afraid of getting hurt again, of letting myself get too attached to you, and yet all along I knew you were the man for me. That I'd never love anyone the way I love you."

"Nor I you, Hayley." He rested his hands on her shoulders and looked deep into her eyes. "You are the most important person in the world to me."

She held him tightly and pressed her face into the fragrant warmth of his neck. "Just don't ever, ever walk out on me again."

"I won't." He kissed her hard, stamping her as his, not just for tonight, but for all time, then warned, "And don't *you* ever start packing."

"I agree, I think I've done that to death," she teased back.

He reached for the papers and tore them in half. "We won't be needing those."

"No. We won't, will we?" Hayley looked just as satisfied as he felt.

"Where's Christine?"

Hayley smiled. "Asleep for the night."

Dillon stroked her hair. "I like her timing."

"She's missed you," Hayley confessed softly.

"I've missed her, too. Almost as much as I've missed you." Dillon kissed her thoroughly. When he finally lifted his head, he saw all the love he'd ever wanted reflected in Hayley's eyes. He knew this relationship was for keeps. It was the way he wanted it.

She slid off his lap.

He stood and swung her up in his arms. "We've wasted enough time," he said huskily, "don't you think?"

"Too much," she agreed as he started for the stairs and the bedrooms upstairs.

"Dillon?"

"What?" he asked as he followed her down onto the mattress and covered her body with his own.

"I'm glad you're home," she whispered, pressing damp kisses in an erotic path down his throat. Deftly her hands undid first his tie, then the buttons on his shirt.

"So am I. And Hayley? This time," he whispered as his mouth drifted down to hers. "This time, it's to stay."

# HARLEQUIN SUPERROMANCE®

## ...there's more to the story!

Superromance. A *big* satisfying read about unforget-
table characters. Each month we offer
*four* very different stories that range from family
drama to adventure and mystery, from highly emo-
tional stories to romantic comedies—and
much more! Stories about people you'll
believe in and care about. Stories too
compelling to put down....

Our authors are among today's *best* romance writ-
ers. You'll find familiar names and
talented newcomers. Many of them are
award winners—and you'll see why!

If you want the biggest and best
in romance fiction, you'll get it
from Superromance!

Available wherever Harlequin books are sold.

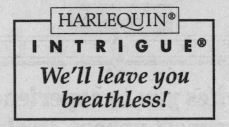

**Harlequin® Historical**

From rugged lawmen and
valiant knights to defiant heiresses
and spirited frontierswomen,
Harlequin Historicals will
capture your imagination with
their dramatic scope, passion
and adventure.

Harlequin Historicals...
they're too good to miss!

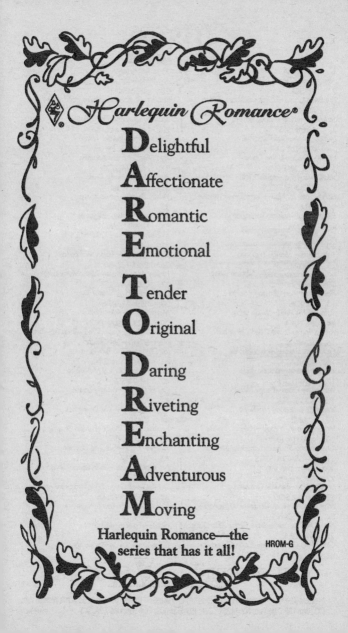

Harlequin Romance®

**D**elightful
**A**ffectionate
**R**omantic
**E**motional

**T**ender
**O**riginal

**D**aring
**R**iveting
**E**nchanting
**A**dventurous
**M**oving

Harlequin Romance—the
series that has it all!

HROM-G

# American HEROES
## AGAINST ALL ODDS

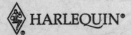

HARLEQUIN®          Silhouette®

Please address questions and book requests to: Harlequin Reader Service U.S.: 3010 Walden Ave.,
P.O. Box 1325, Buffalo, NY 14269 CAN.: P.O. Box 609, Fort Erie, Ont. L2A 5X3          PAHGEN